MUCH ADO ABOUT BENEDICT

Emma Perle

www.emmaperle.com

Cover artwork by www.theoriginalplan.co.uk

For Simon, Samantha and Lucinda who have given me the encouragement to keep writing

CONTENTS

CHAPTER 1

Beatrice

Exasperated I look around at the discarded dresses which lay in crumpled, dejected piles on the floor around me, feeling the pressure to choose something I like. Today is my only chance to find a new dress to wear for a ball my cousin's family are organising in aid of 'Help for Heroes'.

'Does my bum look big in this one?' I swing round trying to catch my rear view in the shop's angled mirrors. Nothing feels quite right today or am I being over critical? 'I wish stock sizes would take into consideration more ample figures!' I say moaning.

Holly, who is providing a steady stream of samples for me to try on, is as ever supportive and encouraging 'you are gorgeous learn to embrace those curves' she says as she finishes securing me into the red gown.

'The grass is always greener Hol – I would give anything for your model's body – everything looks fabulous on you' basically I am envious of her super slim figure.

Holly had decided to stick with the first dress she tried on. An elegant long cream silk shift with spaghetti cross straps and a low v at the back, perfectly complimenting her gorgeous mixed race skin. She didn't want to look too 'showy' as she would be co-hosting the ball being held at her family home in a few weeks' time. That was always her style, not wanting to stand out, even though she is naturally beautiful and would stand out wearing a dustbin bag.

We have grown up together, our fathers are brothers and have always been close. We are only six months apart in age so spent much of our childhood in each other's company. I am lucky, she is like a best friend.

'Red is definitely your colour' she says re-adjusting the laces down the back of the dress 'it's perfect on you' and, standing back to regard me with a critical eye, 'I think this is the one.'

Smoothing down the fabric of the skirt, I present both of my sides to the mirror still not sure.

'Come on Bea, go with the red.' She encourages 'it screams siren and you will be a total knock out'

I am uncomfortable with her reference to me as something alluring, I maintain a work focused ethic and her flattery goes against this. Reluctantly though, I admit to myself, I do quite like the dress, it's a bold choice but I need to be a little more adventurous when it comes to my clothes. 'Ok you have convinced me, I'll get it' I take one more look at myself in the mirror 'anyway I haven't had anything new for a while.'

'Exactly' sounding relieved, she's been really patient with me 'It's been ages since you let your hair down, can't be all work and no play and you deserve some fun.' She reasons as we get dressed back into our clothes. 'We both do. I am excited about the ball. It will be good to meet the guys from the regiment in an off-duty capacity. We get to spend four whole days with them, I can't wait. They'll be just back from overseas and wanting to party!'

'I am looking forward to it' I say 'and will enjoy myself, I just don't need the addition of a man complicating things, single life suits me at the moment.'

Not sure who I am trying to convince.

I have spent the last seven years studying and training both at Cambridge University then at Maurice Spencer Ashwell to gain my admission onto the roll of Solicitors. I'm loving my progression, earning the respect of my peers and learning so much of the world of Corporate Law. I work long hours and take shit from no one, its paying off with the better work coming my way. Throwing complicating curve balls like distracting relationships into the mix is not high on my agenda.

We take our chosen gowns to the boutique store counter. I grab Holly's dress just as we get to the sales clerk. Handing them both over to her I say 'Hi, I'd love to buy this red dress and the cream one but I have just seen their tags. I can't afford both unless you can you can give me some leeway on the price?'

The shop assistant frowns and I can sense Holly shift in discomfort behind me, she always feels awkward when I go into my combative bartering mode.
'Ok if you purchase both dresses I can take 10% off the price'
I look her in the eye 'If you knock 20% off I will definitely take them!'
The shop assistant looks back at me for a moment, looking like she will refuse, then with a reluctant nod she says 'ok, I'll give you a 20% discount.'

'Great thank you so much' I grin delighted with my successful negotiation.

After the dresses have been carefully wrapped up in tissue paper and the bill paid we take the bags and leave the shop. Wandering a short distance down the street we find a café, order some drinks at the counter then sit down at a spare table outside. It is early May, just warm enough to be able to enjoy sitting alfresco and the place is buzzy with chatter from the other customers.

'As you suggested I'm taking Wednesday to Friday off so I can join you all early. How are the preparations going?' I ask as I take a sip of my cappuccino.

'Well, I think. Mum is in overdrive!' she rolls her eyes 'Oh and I meant to tell you, it has a theme, it is going to be a masked ball.' This is a new. 'But don't worry, I know it's short notice, I can ask Mum's dressmaker to make you a mask to match your new dress, she is going to make ours and loads of spares for the men from the regiment, so one extra won't be a problem.'

'I'd really appreciate that, thank you, not sure how I could get one sorted at short notice'

'No problem, let me take a photo of the dress' I reach down to pull it out 'it can stay in the bag, just so she has an idea of the colour'
Holly takes her phone out of her handbag, flips the screen and as she does so a message flashes.
'It's a text, from Ursula ...... brilliant she says she can definitely come to the ball too, she wants to know what we are wearing, hang on I'll let her know ..'

'Remind me who is coming?'

Holly, absorbed in her texting, looks up 'There is an advanced party arriving a couple of days beforehand, like you. My father's crony Major Peter Aragon and some of his officers from the regiment, Captains Claud Florence and Boris Charles and a Captain Mountant ....'

The last name rings a bell and not in a good way. I pale remembering.

Holly continues 'Oh yes and Peter's brother John. I am never sure why my father keeps asking him, he's a bit odd and most unfriendly .....' she glances back at me 'oh my god Bea what's wrong you looked like you have seen a ghost!'

I remember him, I was introduced to him last year. Just the thought of him bothers and angers me. He is perhaps the most infuriating man I have ever met, even more so because he knows he is handsome, panty droppingly so, and he uses that to his advantage at every opportunity.

'You said Captain Mountant – I take it you meant Benedict Mountant?'

'Yes now you mention it I think that is his first name, why?' she eyes me questioningly.

'Ugh I met him last summer at a party hosted by James from the office. He is such a tart, thinks he is 'God's gift' to women, annoyingly handsome but oh my God, he knows it.'

I had been to a barbeque with one of my work colleagues. Some of his old school friends had been invited too, one of them was Benedict. He worked the room seemingly to make it his mission to charm every female there. I didn't giggle and hang onto his every word like the other girls did. He was extremely good looking, tall and dark with sparkly blue eyes but so odiously pleased with himself.

'He's the type who's totally untrustworthy, a different girl every night and relationships are not in his vocabulary. I had overheard him bragging about his conquests to a friend at the time and some bollocks about how we have evolved to eat, drink and have glorious sex.'

It became my mission that afternoon to wipe that smug dimpled smile off his face.

'I refused to be taken in by him, I think he found this quite novel at first, but eventually told me 'not to worry babe, I would be the last on his list anyway''

'Oh' said Holly 'I didn't know about that side of him. Peter speaks highly of his officers and what an amazing team they are.'

I'd had the misfortune of 'bumping into him' more than once after that barbecue. He'd come to meet James for a drink one evening after work in the pub around from our office. I'd coincidently just finished working on a case and was celebrating with some of my team. He'd tried to be all flirty again, which had been rather embarrassing seeing as there was nothing going on between us. It had flustered me in front of my work colleagues, which only added to my contempt of him. Then I had seen him on the Kings Road, when I had been Saturday shopping. I spotted him across the street and hoping I hadn't been seen, dived into a shop to avoid any confrontation. I think he had already clocked me as he came sauntering over trying to be Mr Charming. He took sport in my disdain of him and he just couldn't take the massive all signs blazing message I was giving him that I think he is a total man whore and I am not interested.

I scowl thinking about Benedict Mountant.

'You really don't like him do you?' she giggles 'He's definitely in your bad books, I am intrigued to meet him!'

CHAPTER 2

Benedict

I stumble, bending down on one leg as I am trying quietly to put on my boxer shorts. I pick up my clothes, which are strewn around the floor and tip toe out the bedroom. I do not want to wake the gorgeous Lucinda 'wasn't that her name?' who I'd met the night before. I'd been out celebrating with the regiment and some of us had continued onto a club. Thankfully the working office world had been out to party on a Thursday night. With only one 8 hour day to worry about before the weekend, the club was full till the early hours of the morning. Delightfully full, with lots of 'totty' hanging on to my every word eager to hear about my recent heroics abroad. Lucinda had been the lucky lady who'd caught my eye and I'd gone home with. I'll try to remember to text her later, don't want to be a total douchebag and leave things without saying anything.

My phone buzzes. Grabbing a half empty bottle of water I spy from a table I make my way out of the flat. Pulling the door too I slide my phone to answer.

'Mate where have you been?' Claud's exasperated voice sounds on the line. 'I have been trying to get hold of you, we're leaving in less than an hour!'

'Don't worry I'll be there ..... Lucy was so warm I was waging a war whether to wake her' I hear him groan 'I know, I know, my loyalties lie with you, bros before does, which is why I didn't!'

'You are such a dog! Just don't be late.'

'See you in 50'

I hang up and brake into a jog, if I keep going I will make it back to my flat in 20 minutes from here, I am fit from my army training and anyway it's quicker than trying to find a taxi or relying on public transport. That will give me time for a quick shower and to shove some clothes into a bag before Claud arrives to pick me up.

We are going to stay at the country house of the Colonel's with some of our colleagues a few days before a 'Help for Hero's' ball, a kind of extra thank you for our successful mission abroad.

Thankfully there were no casualties this time. We all came back in one piece and one more fanatic has been successfully captured. He is now sporting an orange jump suite, unable to carry out martyrdom and safely bolted away behind bars.

Showered and packed I pull on my jeans and decide on a light blue polo shirt. I look in the mirror and tousle my hair, casual but not scruffy – I hope it will be appropriate.

A horn sounds outside, I grab my bag and suit carrier and head to the door. Then I stop, it occurs to me to take a gift, so I run back to the kitchen open the fridge and grab a bottle of champagne. I tuck it under my arm, let myself out of the flat and find Claud in his black range rover waiting to take me to the countryside.

'How are you feeling after your 'no hours' sleep and tangle with the hot Lucinda?' he asks as I climb in.

I grin smugly and stretching in the seat reply 'Rejuvenated, refreshed and thoroughly just fucked thank you!' pleasing memories from the night before come to mind. 'Could murder a coffee though, can we stop at the drive through and pick up a takeaway? There's one in a mile or so ..... On me.'

'Yes sure' Claud concentrates on negotiating the traffic.

'How was your evening after I left you?' I ask 'Did Samantha get her wicked way with you?'

He looks sideways briefly, grimaces and shakes his head 'I think Samantha would have eaten me alive! Isn't that what you claimed she did to you the last time we were on leave? You may be my mate but I am not into your sloppy seconds! Anyway I was keen to get some hours of shut eye before our stay at the colonel's. You wouldn't want me falling asleep at the wheel would you?'

'Saving yourself for Mrs Claud to come along or something? '

My friend needed to relax and enjoy what life had to offer a bit more, he was far too principled.

'Talking of which do we know who else will be at the house this weekend?

'The Colonel has a daughter, Holly, I think I met her and the colonel's wife Isniino, when they visited the barracks a while ago. But I was preoccupied with trying to keep the team in check so I don't really remember her. She will be there with some of her friends, joining us for the couple of days before the ball. The Major is arriving when we do along with Boris and I think some of the Major's family.'

'Fill me in on the Colonel's family' I didn't know much about them, had never heard the full story, but was aware of an African link.

'The story I have heard is that when the Colonel was younger he had been with the regiment working in Somalia. Part of the mission was to build a much needed extension to a hospital. Isniino, who is actually the daughter of a Somalian tribal chief, was working as a nurse at said hospital. They fell in love and when the mission was over she returned with him to the UK and they got married. They just have their one daughter, Holly'

◆ ◆ ◆

A couple of hours later, coffees drunk and the world put to rights, we turn onto the long drive up to Messina Hall. The well maintained track winds between open grass parkland dotted with mature estate trees. I can see horses grazing in the late morning sun. After about a quarter of a mile an impressive Georgian cream stone mansion comes into view. Claud parks his range rover on the wide expanse of gravel in front of the house and we get out, grab our bags from the boot and make our way to the front door.

Just as I lift my hand to knock I see two cars speeding up the drive, churning up gravel and dust in their wake. In the first, a silver Aston Martin DB9, I can see Major Peter driving with his brother John in the passenger seat, who I have met a few times.

'Very James Bond!' I mutter but smile and lift my hand in greeting.

The car behind, a navy blue golf, containing our other colleagues and friends Boris and Conrad, skids to a halt next to the Aston Martin. The two men jump out ....

'We nearly had him at the lights!' Conrad exclaims striding towards us.
Boris counters 'I would have taken him' and slapping his hand on Conrad's back 'Conrad here has a lot to learn about combative driving!'

Peter joins them walking to the front door shaking his head

'Boys, Boys behave!'

We embrace in greeting as the front door to the hall opens. Our Colonel stands in the doorway smiling hospitably.

Peter shakes his hand vigorously and says 'Hello my friend, are you braced for this lot to stay?' and turning to us.

'Gentlemen this is our most generous host, Colonel Leopold Uppaugh'

'You are all very welcome' Leo says gesturing us inside 'I have been very much looking forward to your stay with us. And John, it is so good to see you too, I am delighted you agreed to come.'

Leo shakes each of our hands in turn as we introduce ourselves and walk through the door. We enter a huge, high ceilinged hallway, I can't help being impressed. Tall windows either side of the front door let in the views of the valley. It's very grand, but not intimidatingly so, there is still a homely feel inside. A well-worn carpet covers the wide sweeping staircase in front of us, African art hangs on the walls and in the centre of the room on an antique round table stands a large vase of garden flowers; their scent perfuming the air. Behind that, I assume, is Isniino, Leo's wife and their daughter Holly waiting to greet us.

Peter moves towards our hostesses first, hugs Isniino and kisses her on both cheeks.
'Inno so lovely to see you it's been far too long..... And Holly,' he kisses her in greeting 'gosh you are so beautiful and grown up, I can see you are your father's daughter'

Leo beams proudly saying 'so her mother keeps reminding me!'

I am next in line, shaking their hands 'would you have been in any doubt sir?' it jumps out of my mouth before I think about what I am saying.

Leo, however laughs and sparks in return 'given your reputation Mountant and the fact that you were a child when Holly was born, thankfully I am in no doubt that she is actually mine!'

Whoops.

'Come through to the drawing room for a cup of coffee, much needed after your travels' Inno indicates and leads the way, the others shuffle through following her. All except Claud and I who linger, he seems to not want to stop introducing himself to Holly.

Then I see her.

She hovers in the doorway momentarily, looking towards us. Sunlight streams through the window, the beams casting an ethereal halo around her. My breath catches in my throat, I am staring at a beautiful red headed goddess. Absolutely gorgeous with curves in all the right places - ample breasts, small waist and jeans fitting snugly round her hips. I am dumbstruck and can't take my eyes off her.

She steps forward and makes her way towards us.

Recognition dawns, she looks familiar.

A past conquest?

Then I remember, with a jolt, the infuriating woman I met last summer.

Now this could be fun ...

'Oh god look what the cat dragged in!' she drawls as she strides towards us.

I pretend I hadn't heard her and turn my back to her, knowing it will annoy her. Addressing the other two 'sorry did someone just say something?'

She rallies 'I am sure they have more important things to talk about than listen to you.' She joins our group putting her hand out to shake Claud's.

'Hi I'm Beatrice, Holly's cousin'

Claud shakes her hand and looks between us.

'Sorry have you two met?'

'Yes we have had the pleasure, Beatrice' I nod in her direction, then kiss her on each cheek, grinning at her mischievously.

There is silence again Claud looks to Holly, confused, I think they are wondering what on earth is going on.

By way of an explanation I say 'I was looking forward meeting lots of new people this weekend but the first girl I see is the one and only person in the world who does not enjoy my company!'

She counters 'And I will console myself that at least I am doing the rest of the female population a favour. Not having to endure your false charm for a few days', she forces a smile, which is more of a grimace.

'I see you haven't changed since last year. Still have your acid tongue?' I chuckle

'And you clearly haven't gotten any less pleased with yourself!'

Claud and Holly look between us again. There is another silence Beatrice and I are on a glare off, I can feel her contempt of me. Holly grabs her by the arm – 'anyway, the dressmaker has delivered the masks Bea, let's go and see what they are like. Lovely to meet you gentlemen you are welcome to join the others in the drawing room'

She drags Beatrice out of the hallway. Claud turns to me 'What was that hate fuck all about?'

'Oh God I hadn't realised the connection. The first time I met the not so delightful Beatrice was last summer at an old school friend's party. She spent the whole evening calling me on my shit. For some unfounded reason she doesn't like me and we rub each other up, so to speak, the wrong way.'

'Oh' he pauses 'Well that aside, did you notice how drop dead gorgeous Holly is?'

I think about Holly 'Yes she's attractive, not my type though, she's a bit quiet, skinny, not enough woman' I gesture with hands out in front of me 'unlike her feisty friend who could be attractive if it weren't for her spikey personality.' Then thinking of Holly 'She does have a pretty face.'

'I think she is the most beautiful girl I have ever met!' he all but swoons.

'Didn't you meet her before when she visited the Regiment?'

'Yes but I was so preoccupied with work and making sure we made a good impression on the colonel I didn't notice her in that way. Now I am blown away!'

'Brilliant then there is some sport to enjoy this weekend – getting you into bed with the Colonel's daughter'

'Ugh don't be so coarse' his shoulders slump then he smiles 'I don't think she is that sort of girl, a keeper not a sleeper.'

'Oh no, it's too soon mate' I council, he's so impressionable 'Claud you're young and you have your life ahead of you, don't lose your head to the first girl who turns it. I should know.'

Boris comes back into the hallway.

'Are you both going to join us at some stage soon?' he asks

'Just trying to dissuade our friend here from putting all his eggs in one basket'

'What's going on?'

'Young Claudy has a soft spot for the Colonel's daughter'

Boris slaps Claud on the back 'Well if you are going to fall for anyone, it might as well be with the fit, eligible, and only child of one of the wealthiest families in the country!'

CHAPTER 3

Beatrice

Flustered I follow Holly to the kitchen at the back of the house. When we are out of earshot of the men she turns to me.

'You're not wrong about Captain Mountant – he is smoking hot – holy shit!'

'And so bloody conceited' I reply 'now you must see what I am talking about'

'Yup he's definitely hiding horns under that thick dark mane of his'

'Humph don't I know it'

'I like Claud' she states looking a little dreamy

'Yes he seems like a much more genuine person'

'That and other things' Holly giggles and nudges me with her elbow, her eyes sparkle. 'Come on'

On a large well-worn oak table at the end of the room the dress-maker is laying out her work. We walk over to have a look. It is covered with a beautiful array of different coloured masks. Blues, greens, purples, pinks and paler colours shimmer in satins and silks in front of us. Some decorated with an assortment of feathers or edged in beads and some simple plainer ones presumably for the men. They look amazing.

'This must be yours' Holly picks up a bright red silk mask edged with silver piping, large scarlet feathers fan out from the sides. She hands it to me.

'Wow its gorgeous' I hold it in front of my face, trying to catch my reflection in the glass fronted kitchen unit.

'Thank you so much Jane I love it!'

'You're welcome' the dressmaker smiles at me.

We admire the rest on the table, Holly holds up a cream one with pearl beading. 'This must be mine I think' she holds it out in front of her to view, turning it over 'its perfect thank you!'

Holly looks at me 'How are you feeling now after your re-acquaintance with the devil?'

That's definitely one way to look at it 'A little calmer now, thank you' I smile

'Good because I am afraid we've got to go back out front and be sociable again.'

'That's fine I can cope' *I think*

'I'm under orders to show the younger officers, who haven't been here before, around the house, show them their rooms and things. You don't have to come along if you don't feel like it.'

'No I'm good. It's good to get to know them all and we may as well start now.'

She hugs me conspiratorially 'Go girl, give it some sass, you'll be fine.'

We head back to the drawing room towards the sound of coffee cups clinking on saucers and voices chatting. When we enter Inno, seeing us, announces to everyone.

'Holly and Beatrice are going to show you to your rooms and give you a tour of the house, nothing formal, just so you know your way around.'

Everyone looks in our direction smiling. Benedict is looking directly at me and I become a little self-conscious. God what's wrong with me?

Come on Bea do what Holly says 'Sass it out' I plaster a smile on my face and look at everyone else but him.

'And please remember' Inno continues 'While you are here treat the house as your own home. You are here to relax and enjoy yourselves so absolutely no standing on ceremony!'

There is a chorus of thank yous and more smiles.

Holly takes over. 'Would you like to get your bags from the cars and then I can show you upstairs.' Looking directly at Peter she says 'I presume you don't need the tour, you'll be in the blue room where you always used to stay, first room on the left in the west wing. Feel free, if you are happy, to help yourself without having to wait for us.'

Holly and I step back into the hallway, she walks ahead to open the front door. I stay by the table in the centre, looking towards the door. Claud, Boris and Conrad walk through first, Benedict is behind them. By pretending to be fascinated by the flowers I don't have to catch his eye. I feel him walk quite close behind me, it makes me shiver a little and I feel hyper aware, butterflies develop in my stomach.

My eyes go wide. Why is my body reacting in this way to him? Can someone I dislike so much have this effect on me? My pulse rises and I want to scream at myself. He just continues on sauntering through the door and outside as if nothing has happened. So vexatious, I really mustn't let him get to me in the way he does. I've got to rise above my silly female hormones, which at the moment, seem hell-bent on self-destruction.

As the men come back inside we offer to help carry things, they don't need our assistance there aren't any big cases.

Holly starts climbing the stairs 'Let's find your rooms first and then I can show you round the rest of the house.'

She is half way up with the rest of us following. I'm tailing behind last, I need to keep trouble ahead of me where I can see him.

'Damn I forgot the champagne' Benedict stops and announces. He turns to go back nearly knocking me off the step, I plaster myself against the bannister to avoid bumping into him 'Sorry' he says 'I bought a gift for our hosts. Claud chuck me the keys'

Claud fumbles in his pocket and the keys come sailing over our heads and get caught easily by Benedict who is back on the bottom step. He puts his bag and suit carrier down and heads back outside. There is a pause as everyone waits.

'Don't worry I'll wait for him, you all go on and we'll catch you up' I say

'Are you sure Bea?' Holly gives me a pointed look to see if I am really ok with that.

'Yes definitely – he won't be long.'

Against my better judgement I turn back to wait for him in the hallway.

CHAPTER 4

Benedict

I grab the champagne from the drink holder in the passenger door, re-lock the car and turn to see Beatrice waiting just inside the house. The site of her brings a smile to my face, I must play fair, I remind myself. It's just with her I can't seem to leave her be. I can't help myself. Her fiery reactions spur me on further. Seeing her peachy ass hugged in those tight jeans made my fingers itch. I wanted to reach out and pinch her bottom. Imagining her fury at my inappropriate action was too good an opportunity not to enjoy and I chuckle to myself at the thought. But I can't be had up for harassment and I must try to be respectful.

'Thank you for waiting for me' I say as I go back into the house 'I expect you jumped at the chance.'

'Are you serious?' she says 'I did it so the others didn't have to wait. It certainly wasn't out of any benevolence towards you.'

'The best bit now' I say turning to her just inside the door 'is you get to show me my bedroom..... all on our own!' I raise my eyebrows in comic anticipation. She has the decency to look appalled.

'You are so deluded. If you think for one moment that that thought is anything other than abhorrent to me, then you are more of a fool than I first took you for.'

I put a hand out and trace my finger down her arm. 'Come on

don't tell me you have never thought about it.' She stills for just a second and then looks at me shocked.

Bingo I say to myself *so there is a chink in Boudica's armour.*

Then she shrugs away. Just at this moment Pete comes out of the drawing room and catches the last second of Beatrice shrugging away from me. He looks towards me questioningly and frowns a little, time to behave myself.

'Mountant a word please!'

Beatrice takes her chance. 'I'll see how they're getting on in the kitchen. You'll find the others upstairs just head off to the left when you reach the top.'

She bolts, leaving me to my telling off.

CHAPTER 5

Benedict

After a lecture from Pete about my conduct whilst I am here I collect my bag and suit carrier that I had dumped at the bottom of the stairs. I climb back up and turn left at the top as Beatrice had told me to. Walking past a couple of closed bedroom doors I see that somebody had efficiently put post-it notes on them to indicate who is sleeping where, I find mine towards the end of the corridor.

I open the door and walk into my bedroom. It is impressive for a guest room. A large four poster bed, covered in a fur throw, dominates the room. The bed linen shows crisp and white underneath. To the side of the bed is a door to the en-suite, dumping my bag on the bed I go to the bathroom. It has a wet-room style shower and grey marble topped sink unit. I splash some water on my face and check out my reflection in the mirror. Thinking of Beatrice, whose anger makes me horney, my dick stirs and I smile involuntarily. *Stop Benedict this is not helping* – I squeeze some soap from the dispenser and try to wash away those arousing thoughts as I scrub my face. I towel dry my face as I wander back round the bed to gaze through the window which gives an expansive view of the rear of the house. Directly below I look down on an arbour covered in vines with some seating underneath. There is a swimming pool to the right and then further off a tennis court and what looks like a maze made with tall box hedging. Lucky us, it is going to be a good few days.

Venturing back downstairs I hear the conversational buzz of the others. I follow the sound which leads me to the orangery and join my colleagues. Floor to ceiling windows show off an immaculate parterre outside. French doors open out to a path which leads to the swimming pool. Inside there are some small citrus trees in pots and a few comfortable looking sofas. Along the back wall, on a long table, a buffet lunch has been laid out for us. I grab a plate and follow Peter and Claud as we help ourselves to the delicious looking food.

'Hi Mate I was wondering where you had gotten to' Claud says to me.

'Yeah sorry I went for an explore around the house on my own and found where I am sleeping – cool rooms'

Pete puts a chunk of bread on his plate and grabs a glass of beer, we do the same and follow him outside. We find the table, laid up with knives, forks and napkins, under the arbour I had seen from my bedroom window.

As we sit down and start our lunch Pete starts talking.

'What happened to you both earlier when you disappeared before coffee?

'I couldn't drag Claud away from the girls. He was quite taken with one in particular' I tease and elbow Claud who scrunches his eyes closed looking awkward.

'Come on who with?' Pete looks between us

'Our charming hostess, Holly' I say 'appears the interest could be mutual'. Pete raises his eyebrows and looks to Claud for verification.

Claud reddens a little. 'If Ben says so then I hope it's true'

Pete laughs 'well that's great news, you couldn't fall for anyone better, just as long as you behave like a gentleman to her. Ben, given your extensive knowledge of the fairer sex, I assume you give good counsel?'

Given that relationships are not in my repertoire this makes me chuckle.

'Not me, I am the last person he should be turning to. As you know long term love is not my thing, there are too many fishes in the sea for me to hook up with. You are better qualified Pete at courting than I am.'

Pete takes a sip of his beer 'Ah but you just haven't met the right person yet – I predict when you do you will fall harder than any of us!'

Yeah right

'Anyway enough about me. It's Claud who needs the strategy of pulling the wool over Holly's eyes and convincing her he is worthy.'

Peter turns his full attention on Claud and I tune out.

My subconscious causes the hair to raise on the back of my neck. I turn in my seat, aware of her presence before I see her, Beatrice comes outside with a plate of food. She has changed from her jeans and looks gorgeous in a pale green summer dress, it accentuates her curves – I watch her mesmerised, why does she do this to me? She is with Holly but it is only her I want to watch. She is smiling as she looks around for somewhere to sit. Then she catches me looking at her, her smile drops and she glares at me. She ushers Holly in the opposite direction to some seats by the pool, looking over her shoulder one more time she scowls at me and then turns back and laughs at something she says.

'If something hasn't happened before the party on Friday we have the perfect opportunity of creating a ruse. We will all be in masks so partially disguised. I will have a think and come up with a master plan to both put a good word in for you, and create a diversion, so the two of you can enjoy some alone time.

What do you recon Mountant? Operation Claud and Holly … anything to add?' Pete looks at me questioningly as I zone back in.

'Er no … sounds like you have it covered … all good though'

We hear a squeal coming in the direction of the girls. Looking round we see Beatrice leap out of her seat and run up to give a hug to an older gentleman who has just arrived. He looks familiar. Then the Colonel comes out to join them and I see their resemblance, he must be his brother Tony. Holly gives Tony a hug and the four are engaged in animated conversation.

I see Claud staring at Holly with a goofy smile on his face.

Oh bloody hell.

Then Pete standing up, says to us both 'If we've all finished why don't we go and introduce ourselves to the Colonel's brother.'

CHAPTER 6

Beatrice

After lunch and catching up with my father this afternoon, I feel that I need a bit of time on my own. I detour on my way back from the swimming pool to the kitchen and find Inno instructing the cook and supper already starting to be prepared. I offer to help but everything is under control. I turn to leave the kitchen.

'I'll just head back up to my room to sort my stuff out, I haven't unpacked properly yet and I need to hang up my dress.'

'Of course, do you want to take your mask?' I collect it from the table and walk back to the door 'Take your time. I'll get Holly to give you a shout later when supper is ready' Inno calls after me.

'Thank you' I reply as I make my way out of the kitchen and up the back stairs.

Wandering to my bedroom, in the dimly lit east wing, I can still hear the hum of voices coming from outside and downstairs. As I get to my bedroom door my heel catches on the corner of a rug. It makes me trip and I fall forward dropping the mask. Out of nowhere unseen hands reach out and grab my arms, I shriek. Straightening up I come face to face with a broad chest. I gasp, shocked and flustered as I hadn't seen anyone coming. Embarrassed that someone witnessed me tripping I am blushing and as my gaze travels upwards it locks into the steely blue eyes of Benedict.

Indignation swiftly follows and I try to shrug him off.

'Excuse me' I say

He maintains his hold of my arms, his eyes piercing through me and I feel my heart beat quicken. His touch sears into my skin, every nerve ending alive to the sensation and I am no longer able to pull away. My body is reacting to him in a way I can't ignore and I stare at him in disbelief.

This is so wrong but I can't help myself. We continue to stare at each other transfixed. It feels as if time has frozen, our only awareness is this unfounded connection like electricity is coursing between us. His eyes slowly lower and as he looks at my lips, I involuntarily lick them..... WHY did I do that? Then his eyes move down towards my breasts, I feel exposed and my traitorous nipples harden visibly through the thin fabric of my dress. He lifts one eyebrow questioningly.

'Oh – no way!' I huff

Realisation and horror at myself at what is happening brings me to my senses and I pull away. I make it through my bedroom door. Benedict is right behind me. His strong arms grasp me and he turns me around.

My door swings closed, the crashing sound reverberates through the walls around us. Before I can react further his lips slam onto mine. Before I can think rationally I kiss him back, our tongues wage war in a frenzy consumed by the moment. Against all my principles I am unable to stop my body in responding this way. Desire, heat and sensation take over, all rational thought leaving my brain. It is not supposed to feel so good.

We continue our delirious kissing, my mind screaming to stop what I am doing, but I can't. I cannot deny the craving hunger that has possessed me.

Pulling apart and panting for a moment we just stare at each other in silence, the only noise to be heard is the tic toc of the grandfather clock on the landing and the distant chatter of the other guests.

Benedict reaches out and featherlike runs a finger down the side of my neck and across my shoulder, I shiver spontaneously, it continues its path down to my breast and circles one nipple which immediately pebbles to attention and I feel a glow in my core. We look into each other eyes.

'Do you want me to stop?' He asks

Yes this can't go any further 'No'

'Take your dress off' he authoritatively demands. It is as if I'm in a trance, against my rational conscious, I lift my dress up and slowly over my head.

His gaze travels over my torso and his fingers stroke leisurely across my collar bone. I feel exposed as goose bumps erupt over my body, I shiver and a yearning to be touched all over consumes my mind.

Benedict traces his finger down my stomach and gently teases the lace on the edge of my panty.

I gasp.

Heat pools between my legs. I look down and seeing the bulge in his jeans know that he is as captivated by this moment as I am.

He guides me gently backwards towards the bed and as the back of my legs meet the edge I fall backwards. He appears over me and rests one muscular arm on the mattress beside me.

'Just perfect' he admires my body 'I want to play with you, and you'll come hard for me.' He rolls one of my nipples between his finger and thumb through the fabric of my bra, it puckers. 'I'll want to fuck you too... but not now.' He rubs my other nipple in the same way, the textured lace adding to the friction, my senses are on overload. 'But you should know when we do fuck, you will be seeing stars and I will ruin you for anyone else'

His dirty words turn me on. His fingers stroke purposefully up and down my inner thighs. My senses at their peak, the strokes like fireworks on my skin as they gradually make their way higher and higher, as they graze the underside of my panties my insides constrict sweetly. He moves the fabric aside circling my clit a few times. I start to pant and he plunges his finger inside me, expertly exploring, putting pressure and massaging against my most sensitive areas, then he adds another finger and the extra fullness makes me moan in ecstasy.

'Fuck you're wet' he says keeping up the momentum. His fingers move in and out caressing my g-spot, it makes me want more. I look down and see myself near naked while he is fully clothed. It makes me feel so wanton. I don't want him to stop.

I still can't believe what is happening. Looking at Benedict's tortured face and the questions in his eyes I believe he shares my anguish.

Why do we do this to each other?

My body tightens with the anticipation of an orgasm, he senses this and withdraws his fingers. It makes me whimper at the loss of friction. He smiles smugly. Then he takes hold of my panties and pulls them down and off. He gets down on his knees before me, guides my thighs apart and I feel the sensation of the cooler air on me.

For a moment humiliation makes me resist and I try to sit up. He puts a hand on my stomach.

'Stay' he says, his voice so deep and commanding, I obey, its effect liquefies my insides increasing my need.

He inhales deeply,

'You smell delicious'

He ducks down and begins an assault on my clitoris with his tongue, circling and sucking. He is so good at this, it feels amazing. He buries his head deeper and moves his tongue and in out of me resting on the point just in front of my clitoris, his onslaught continues, when I think I can't take it anymore he delivers gentle featherlike bites. The sensation is too much, so intense. I arch my back as light travels up my spine and down my limbs, I orgasm deliciously, cry out and my body voluntarily bucks; taken over by the all-consuming pleasure coursing through me. I feel like I am suspended. I lie still with my eyes closed and enjoy the moment, the aftershocks abate slowly feeling wonderful.

Benedict stares at me transfixed.

All too soon, footsteps in the hallway interrupt my post orgasmic haze, it brings us both to our senses and we freeze. I recognise Holly's voice on the other side of my door.

'Oh there is a mask!

I register the sound of her approach and she knocks three times on the door. Benedict puts his fingers to his lips and dashes to the en-suite bathroom.

'Bea are you in there, you must have dropped your mask?'

I quickly scramble back on the bed and dive under the duvet as the door slowly opens.

'Bea are you there?' Holly sees me in bed and moves towards me 'Bea are you ok?'

I yawn, I hope convincingly, 'sorry yes fine, just needed a quick snooze and the bed looked so comfy' I stretch my arms and yawn again hoping to make it look like I have just been woken.

Holly's eyes travel across the room and she sees my dress strewn across the floor and the panties next to the bed, she giggles.

'Seems like sleeping wasn't the only thing you needed!' She looks at me in amusement but I don't react, I don't want to give myself away. 'Anyway sorry' she stammers 'I have been sent to find you. Supper is being served soon, very relaxed, but didn't want you to miss out.' She lingers by the door and looks round the room one more time, she appears perplexed and frowns. Then she shakes her head as if to shoo away a thought 'Anyway I'll leave you to it and see you downstairs' She walks out and shuts the door behind her.

I fall back on my pillow, my hands over my face and groan, I am mortified.

What just happened?

The en-suite door opens and Benedict peeks round and starts moving towards the bed. As he nears me, I hold up a flat hand to stop him.

'Just go!'

'I think the coast is clear' ignoring me and smirking he continues his advance. 'It's my turn now'

I sit up and glare at him, defensively holding the duvet up over my breasts 'I don't know what you think is going on but this should never have happened. I don't even like you and certainly don't want to be yet another notch on your bedpost'. As I speak, there is a betraying thought which doesn't want to send him off. I am furious at myself for entertaining any such notion and push the feeling away.

Benedict pouts like a naughty school boy.

'Please go! We only have a short time till supper and I need to compose myself. We must forget this episode ever happened.'

He looks at me for a second, as if in deliberation

'If that is what you want.'

He falters again as if there is a possibility I will change my mind. I glare at him and gesture my head towards the door, resolute. He gives in.

'Ok then we'll put this down to a moment of madness and I will take my blue balls and go elsewhere'

Benedict takes one more moment to stare at me. As I start to turn away from him I see him run a hand through his unruly hair then he spins rounds and walks out of the room.

CHAPTER 7

Benedict

I make my way from Beatrice's bedroom, shit what just happened? I did seek her out earlier but just to see if we could come to some sort of truce. I didn't want our sparing to create an atmosphere while we are guests of the Uppaughs. Not only that but, as Pete reminded me, I could be up for Major next year and I don't want to create a bad impression of my conduct especially in the company of some of the regiment. Even though we are here to relax and enjoy ourselves I still have to behave.

I knew I was misbehaving, using my stealth tactics to surprise her. I hadn't waited long before she appeared outside her room, I was hidden in the next doorway and the dim lighting helped me to stay in the shadow. The tempting idea to put her 'off-balance' by surprising her and giving me the upper hand for our chat had been last minute but I had taken the opportunity. When I caught her from falling I could feel an electric connection between us. It was like my hands had fused to her arms, just touching her felt so good I didn't want to let her go. Then her looking into my eyes, just before she recognised me, I wanted to hold that moment, she is so beautiful ... but oh God so challenging.

I know Beatrice doesn't think very highly of me – I don't know exactly why she takes such issue. Her apparent aversion to me fuels my competitive nature though. She drives the hell out of me – she is so feisty and so confrontational! Fuck though she's hot – I couldn't stop myself. But I must. I know myself and my commitment issues, and she is the Colonels niece, I don't want to shit on my own doorstep. I must leave her alone.

I make my way back to my bedroom. Taking a shower and with it the need to wash away the aroma of Beatrice from myself both physically and metaphorically, I let the water cascade over me and try to concentrate on other things. My mind keeps going back to the memory of her creamy white skin and the way she cried out when she came, my diversional tactic to shower is futile as my erection returns. I turn the water to cold, its chilling temperature shocks me but at least my cock has the decency to abate as the blood withdraws back into my body. I shiver a little as I climb out and wrap a towel around me.

I pull chinos and a button down linen shirt out of my bag to smarten myself up a bit for supper. Cleaning my teeth and spraying on some aftershave I look in the mirror, slick my hair back with my hands and start to feel a little more respectable. I step into my loafers and then exit my bedroom, following the sound of voices back down the front stairs to the drawing room.

On entering Leo offers me a gin and tonic, thanking him I savour the first sip and take a look around as he busies himself making another one for the next arrival. Boris and Conrad are chatting conspiratorially in the corner so I decide to find out what bollocks they are coming up with and join them.

'Oh hi Ben just discussing cars'

Whooppeee I inwardly groan, I prefer bike chat so I suppose I'm no better.

While they are discussing Pete's DB9 I take a look around the room. Beatrice is talking to Inno and her father a few feet away from me, she is looking sensational in a green and gold African print halter neck maxi dress, the neckline plunges down deep into her cleavage and her red hair is loose and falling over her shoulders. I want to stay staring at her, captivated with the way her lips move as she talks and laughs, but I force myself to concentrate on the boys and not taunt her any further by being caught gawping. She doesn't look my way at all, her resolve evidently stronger than mine.

We aren't seated near each other during supper, I can see her across the table and sometimes she scowls at me which makes me want to laugh out loud. She is gorgeous even when she is angry but I stay on best behaviour and give her the space she asked for.

Later on I join the boys for snooker, we stay up till the early hours drinking whisky and playing out our little tournament. It's really good being able to relax away from the regiment and enjoy each other's easy company under our own terms. Staying at the Uppaugh's means there is no threat of early wake up runs or paperwork to keep a clear head to the following day, typical of life in the army. I fully intend to enjoy all the facilities that Messina Hall has to offer, we are lucky to be guests here and even if I have to leave Beatrice alone, I will make the most of my stay.

CHAPTER 8

Beatrice

I roll over and feel the warmth of a small ray of sun peeping through the curtain on my face. As I come to, I stretch out and pull the soft duvet round me more snugly, it is deliciously cosy in bed. Wondering what time it is I reach out to my phone on the bedside table angle it towards me and see that it is just after 7 am. *Hmm early still I can doze for a bit longer.*

My eyes close again, remembering last night's supper. Thankfully I had been sat away from Benedict so we didn't have to pretend to be nice to each other. I kept catching his eye though and we got into that annoying game when you just subconsciously check to see if they are not looking at you and they catch you doing it. Ugh - even more annoying was that he found it amusing and I had to suffer the smug smile when he caught me. Claud and Holly sat next to each other and talked all evening, must have been boring for the person on their other sides. I'm pleased for her though he seems really nice.

I become aware of the sound of gentle splashing, listening to its rhythm it sounds like someone is up for an early morning swim. After a few minutes of listening my legs involuntarily swing themselves over the side of the bed and I saunter to the window, push the curtain a little aside and peek down to see who it might be. I see strong muscular arms make light work through the water and dark hair swish as the swimmer moves his head to take a breath every other stroke. I feel a buzz of adrenaline low in my groin and acknowledge deep down it is Benedict.

I can't tear my eyes away from watching.

Standing rooted to the spot I watch him front crawl back and forth eating up lengths of the pool, he is like an Olympic swimmer, his pace relentless.

Then he stops at one end, stands up and flicks the hair out of his eyes. He takes a few deep breaths then launches himself up the steps and out of the pool.

I gawp. He has the perfect body. His chest is ripped, and my eyes drink in his defined stomach muscles. There is no chest hair just a small glory trail leading lower down to his trunks, which wet, cling to him and allude to his size underneath. He has the body of an Adonis. Despite the fact that he knows he is handsome, I can't help myself and feast on the sight below my window.

He lifts a towel from next to the pool and reaches up with it to scrub his hair. Stretching and rippling more muscles as he does so he leans slightly backwards as he dries the back of his head. He is glorious and I stare reverently.

He brings the towel back down over his face and, as if aware of my presence, he stares up at my window. Our eyes lock. We stare at each other for a few moments then a slow knowing smile crawls across his face.

I react next, *oh shit!* Mortification at what I have been caught doing floods through me. I drop the curtain spin round and throw my back against the wall, as if trying to hide. *What have I done!* I can feel the shame coursing through me as I blush from my head to my toes.

I stomp away from the wall and pace back and forth my head in my hands.

Shit shit shit I am such an idiot!

I hear purposeful footsteps outside in the hall. Then my bedroom door bursts open and gets banged shut as Benedict strides in towards me wearing nothing but the towel from the pool.

'Jesus Christ! You can't just barge in he....'

His mouth smashes onto mine.

Oh no, no way not this time!

I try to pull away and push against his still damp chest. I meet solid unyielding muscle, my efforts futile as he continues his assault. My body has other ideas. My lips return his kisses, our tongues wrangle with each other and my arms, against reasoning, reach up around the back of his neck and my nails bury themselves in his shorn hair there. He moans in pleasure against my mouth.

He reaches down under my short nightie and thrusts two fingers inside me. I groan, my body giving me away, I am even wetter than before. He fucks me with his fingers rubbing his thumb against my clit. I can't get enough.

It drives me wild.

I want more ...

'I want you inside me.' I pant. 'Now!' Oh my treacherous body, yet again pleasure has ridden roughshod over my principle.

'No problem' he whips his towel away from him and I see for the first time how glorious his cock is. Long and thick a few pronounced veins running down its length. I reach out and rub my hand up and down, it is rock velvet to touch. My thumb circles in the bud of pre cum at its peak. He groans and manoeuvres me back to the wall.

'Condom?'

'In the drawer - just there' I stammer and indicate to the dressing table next to us.

He opens the drawer with one hand, feels for the foil packet then brings it up and rips it open with his teeth. He slides it down snugly round his erection.

'Put your arms around my neck'

I do as I am told and lift my arms. In one movement he lifts my nightie up around my waist and raises me, thrusting deep inside.

My legs wrap around him and my core spontaneously clenches him inside me, he growls predatorily. He starts to move hard and fast in and out of me.

I know the door is not locked and we could be found out at any time but at this moment I don't care. I need to get him out of my system. To encourage him further I bite into his neck. He hisses. Then I deliver little nips up to and on his earlobe. It drives him wild and his pace increases.

My need builds and I feel my body convulsing, I meet every one of his thrusts, it is all consuming. Then deep in my stomach a sublime tightening.

'I'm coming'

'Stay with me' he pants as he stabs deep into me. Then with one final intense thrust he comes hard and his body stills, his dick pulsing inside me.

My orgasm crashes through me, my mind on another plain as my back arches and I moan in bliss. The delicious throbbing continues as I slump my head against his shoulder.

We stay like that connected and I can feel the beat of his heart against my chest.

He gently lifts me off him and places me back on the floor. He removes the condom, knots it, folds it in a tissue and throws it in the bin. I look into his eyes, I am still panting a little. He smiles and it lights up his whole face showing his dimples to their full effect and his eyes twinkle. Damn he is gorgeous.

Then he turns round picks up his towel from the floor and wraps it around himself. He looks back at me and starts to walk towards the door. Just as he puts his hand out to the door knob he turns his head back.

'Thank you, that was fantastic....... Now I think we are even'

What?

He winks at me and strides out of the bedroom.

I respond in shock to his departing back, my voice incredulous 'You're such an asshole .... and a crap lay!'

The door closes behind him and I am left fuming. I breathe deep huffing breaths my anger palpable in the room as if a red mist is surrounding me. I am so furious I don't know what to do with myself.

I stomp backwards and forwards, sit on the bed and then stand up, unable to process my ire. Ugh he has got the better of me again. Why oh why am I such an idiot!

Calm down Beatrice, this wasn't intended, you knew he was a prize prick. Just put it down to a great lay and move on.

Ok one foot in front of the other, irate thoughts still circling my brain, I make my way to the bathroom and turn on the shower. As I step under the drencher head I squirt soap onto my hand and rub it into a lather frantically all over me. Twice between my legs.

Oh how could I be so reckless?

I shampoo my hair eager not to leave any trace of that man on me. Why did it feel so right then and so wrong now? And I ordered him to fuck me! As I massage the shampoo into my head

I relax and start to reconcile with myself. The gentle movement of my fingers offering some comfort, it reminds me of scratching the back of his neck. He seemed to like that, it had made him moan in pleasure I will remember that .... What? Where did that come from? No way will I remember anything .... And absolutely NO WAY is he EVER coming so close like that to me again!

Pull yourself together Beatrice, put on your prettiest dress, plaster a smile on your face and own your morning.

Right action – time to put 'Mr Mountalot' to a distant memory. Despite myself I giggle at my own version of his name.

CHAPTER 9

Beatrice

I join a group of the men for breakfast. 'Morning' I smile to everyone sitting, I take a place between my father and Leo and help myself to some coffee. Good I can take my mind off my earlier encounter, no sign of trouble here. I'll try to get to know the other guests; John, Conrad and Boris are also seated and talking amongst themselves.

My father smiles at me fondly as I sit down. 'Morning darling I hope you slept well' He takes a sip of his coffee 'I've been catching up on the gossip'

Leo, through a piece of croissant 'Ooh good, anything interesting we should know about?'

'Well' he pauses for effect 'I have heard that young Captain Florence has taken a shine to your daughter AND means to declare himself tomorrow night at the ball.'

Leo swallows and sits up 'And how reliable is your source of this piece of news?'

'I can't divulge my source.' You've probably heard the same Bea?' They both turn to me questioningly and I am happy to focus on my lovely cousin instead of my own plight.

'She does in deed seem rather smitten when there is any mention of Claud' I don't want to give too much away but I know she genuinely likes him and I am really happy for her. He seems to have honourable intentions towards her, unlike his bloody friend, so it's promising for them. Plus they are goofy and slightly awkward in each other's company, I take that as a sign they have feelings for each other.

'I like him, he seems a decent chap' Leo muses then looking at me 'Have you seen Holly yet this morning?'

'Err not yet. Do you need her for anything? I can go and see if she is still in her room'.

'No don't worry you've just sat down' he swigs down the rest of his coffee, pushes his chair back and stands 'I wanted to talk to her about the tennis activity this afternoon. I take it you will play?'

'Yes of course I am looking forward to it'

'Great I'll see you later' he leaves the breakfast room.

As I help myself to some toast and start buttering it, I listen to the other men's conversation. They are also discussing Claud and his pining after Holly. Boris appears to be the one with the knowledge, John is particularly interested.

I study the dynamic between them. Conrad is fussing around John offering and passing him things and he seems to like the attention. Plus their body language is focussed towards each other, John has his arm on the back of Conrad's chair. Conrad laughs at something he says and I spy, as his head falls forward, that he touches John's knee. It could be an innocent moment of comradeship but I wonder if there is more to it and there something going on between them?

'I heard from Pete that he assisting Claud in his dating endeavour at the ball tomorrow night' Boris draws their attention back to his hot topic.

Conrad yawns and John says, slightly sarcastically

'Well I'm delighted for the happy couple, and what more could they want than my brother's interference' he pushes his chair back and stands up 'Conrad are we partnering at the tennis later?'

Conrad leaps to his feet 'yes that would be great'

John addresses all of us 'I'll join you all later' he nods at no one in particular then turns, disappearing from the breakfast room, purposefully on his own, leaving Conrad still standing and watching his departing back.

CHAPTER 10

Beatrice

Holly and I are partnering for tennis. We are going to play against Uncle Leo and my father. It is a warm sunny afternoon with a few whispy clouds strewn across the sky and a gentle breeze warm and soothing. I am wearing my tennis dress, heavy duty sports bra and some tennis shorts. Holly is in a crop top and skort – I always feel somewhat elephantine in her company.

We warm up on our own before the men arrive, hitting balls back and forth to each other. I am impressed with Hol, despite her petite frame she is a surprisingly strong player. We practise a few serves to each other and then meet on the edge of the court for a drink of water. Over by the house I see our fathers making their way here in their white tennis outfits, with slightly retro style shorter shorts, they look kind of cool.

'I overheard Boris gossiping with John and Conrad that he knows that Claud has a soft spot for you and was going to make an advance tomorrow night' I relay to Holly

'Oh God' she groans 'well that's jinxed it if everyone knows now nothing will ever happen. It's too contrived!'

Poor Holly, I know Claud is as keen as mustard, but when you want something so badly your self-esteem waivers and you can't believe the other will feel the same way as you do.

'It will be fine I promise' I give her a hug. 'By the way changing the subject how well do you know John?'

'Not that well, only as Peter's brother and what I hear through him' she puts her head on one side thinking. 'There was some trouble with him a year or so ago, I'm not sure exactly what but there was a falling out in the family. I think it's resolved now though.'

Thinking of his actions earlier. 'My 'gaydar' was on high alert at breakfast, I think there is something going on between him and Conrad.'

'Noooooo! Oh my god that's such a good spot! What makes you think that?'

I recount what I saw.

'Oh goodie I love a romance I'm going to keep my eye out for that one even if it is with grumpy John!'

'Hi girls' we are joined by Leo and my Dad. 'We need a bit of a warm up – shall we get going so as not to hold up the other match?'

The four of us knock up and then get into our match enjoying the friendly rivalry. During the game the next pairings arrive, John and Conrad, they sit down next to the court to watch us. They are seated on some cushioned garden furniture lined up in front of the tennis hut.

I become self-conscious, I can see in my peripheral vision that Benedict has arrived with Claud and I can feel him watching me. He hampers my concentration, a couple of times I miss hit the ball and it goes sailing high out of the court. I can hear him snicker so I huff and shoot him a dirty look. He winks back at me.

Ugh he is so odious!

I try to concentrate on the game but our fathers gain the upper hand on our tie break and narrowly beat us. The four of us meet at the net and Leo and my Dad shake our hands then kiss us on each cheek. Holly is complimenting them on their game as we leave the court.

I am just through the court gate as the next four walk towards us to start their game. Benedict is talking tactics to Claud but as we pass his arm lightly brushes against mine. A thousand vaults shoot up my arm and all over me. I look up at him a little stunned. Benedict reacts too and our eyes meet. A ghost of confusion crosses his face and he stalls ever so slightly. Then Claud says something replying to his earlier comment, and he turns his focus back to his friend as they continue on to the court.

While little fire crackers are still diffusing themselves through my body I sit down on one of the chairs facing the court. Holly hands me a glass of lemonade. I take it smiling in thanks. My mind is a jumble of conflicting emotions. How can I dislike someone so much and yet have such a physical reaction to him. He is the last person on the planet I would ever consider partner material and yet he makes my body feel in ways I didn't even know I was capable of. It is clear we have a connection but in body only, certainly not minds. Thank goodness we can go our separate ways after the weekend, I can go back to the work I love and won't need to dwell on him ever again. Any yet why does that thought needle a tiny feeling of bereftness?

'Ugh' I say out loud by mistake

Holly's eyes shoot from watching predominantly Claud and she gives me a look of concern 'Are you ok?'

'Good Shot!' Leo claps and we all revert our gaze back to the game.

Claud is looking pleased with himself as Benedict announces. 'Love fifteen' and pats him on the back. They resume their positions to accept a serve from John.

'Benedict's a fun chap' Leo states to the rest of us.

'Humph he would be if he wasn't so damn pleased with himself all the time' I counter

Leo laughs 'Oh niece you definitely take no prisoners. Has anyone caught your eye this week?'

I nearly spit out my lemonade, redden guiltily and reply a little flustered 'oh no ... you know me, I am married to my work Uncle Leo'

Holly looks at me curiously.

Dad exclaims 'Our Holly is a spirited one. It will take quite a man to tame her or put up with her sharp tongue'

'I am sure she will find someone one day who will make her happy, in fact I know she will' Uncle Leo says

They continue to discuss my prospects or lack of as marriage material. I know they mean well but it is a little frustrating, just old fashioned I suppose, the world has changed a lot since they were younger

Leo then turns his attention to Holly 'Claud's a good man, I hear you have quite caught his eye'

God this conversation is like something out of a Shakespeare comedy. If my father and uncle could hear themselves discuss the men and our marriage prospects they might appreciate how out of the dark ages it sounds.

'Holly your mother asked me to see if you would be able to help her finalise the table plans for tomorrow night. Would you pop by the kitchen and give her a hand?' Leo gets up to go. 'Come on Tony we can have the first showers before all the hot water goes!'

The three of them start to head back to the house 'Would you like me to lock up the tennis hut when the match is finished?' I call to Leo

'Ah yes that would be helpful thank you Beatrice. I'll see you at supper' He re-joins my father and Holly.

The match finishes and the men shake hands at the net. It is my cue to stand up and start packing up the seat cushions and gather the empty glasses back into the hut.

CHAPTER 11

Benedict

Nothing better than a good tennis game, especially when you win. Losing seems to sour John's mood even more and I take some delight in that, like poking the bear, he is a miserable sod and I still can't believe he is Pete's brother, they are polar opposites.

Pete has spent his lifetime being understanding, supportive and loyal to his half-brother John. John, on the other hand, has spent his lifetime with a potato field size chip on his shoulder. Pete's parents are aristocrats, Lord and Lady Aragon, his mother Jane had had a relationship before she married. John was about two years old, I think, when Jane married Lord Aragon but he has grown up as one of the family, Lord Aragon treating him like his own. The only sticking point for John is that Pete is the true heir and will inherit the title and estate. John has never forgiven his brother for that.

Beatrice is packing up the stuff when our match finishes. Watching her play tennis was mesmerising, I couldn't take my eyes of the way her boobs bounced as she moved around the court. My mind was on 'slo-mo' glued to watching them reverberate two or three times a go as she leapt to take a shot or return a backhand. And the fascinating way her skirt lifted, giving her tennis knickers a cameo, when she served or volleyed a ball revealing more of her glorious thighs. I had a semi through most of her match. Served her right when she fluffed a few shots, if she knew the frustrations my dick was enduring just at the sight of her jumping around, she would appreciate she wasn't the only one with misbehaving balls.

After we knocked into each other before my match, I could feel that connective buzz we have. It makes me want to come back for more, an alien reaction for me, it is both surprising but intriguing.

As I leave the court with the boys, we see Beatrice disappearing inside the hut with an armful of seat cushions.

'I'll see if she needs a hand. You all go on and I'll catch up with you back at the house'
Unsuspecting, and probably relieved that they don't have to do a job, there is a round of

'Thanks mate' 'see you later' 'see you at supper' and they wander back to the house.

I steel myself, I know I was a dick to her earlier, and will have to do some grovelling. I have surpassed my previous performances with my wanker behaviour and am not especially proud of myself. I take a deep breath, grab a couple of glasses from the table and follow her into the hut.

She knows I am behind her as I see her stiffen ever so slightly, plus the glasses clink audibly when I put them down. Ignoring me she starts to stack the cushions in a pantomime staccato way into a bench stored by the wall.

'We both know I am here' I start with

She sighs audibly

Doh Benedict just to piss her off even more

'Sorry I didn't mean that, I came to apologise for earlier.' I begin grovelling 'I know it was a douchebag thing to do, marching out on you like I did.'

She stands up and turns to look at me. She looks mighty pissed off.

'Actually I am more cross with myself. I know what you are like and it's all a game, I am a game, to you.' She pauses 'Having said that I didn't realise you could go to quite such lengths'

'I know, believe me I am particularly ashamed of myself'

'Humph. Look I knew what I was getting myself into, apology accepted and all that. You are just a prick and I have learnt my lesson now.'

One of the cushions, which had just been stacked, rebelliously falls off the top of the pile, she turns round and bends down to pick it up, huffing and puffing. As she reaches down her skirt raises up and I get the front row view of those big tennis knickers. I am done for. My fingers twitching with a will of their own, reach forward and stroke the top of her thigh. She spins round.

'What do you think you are doing?' horror etched on her face.

My hand flies back to me as if it has been burnt 'Oh God sorry I can't help myself.' I try another tact 'I can't ignore that there is a chemistry between us, when we knocked arms by the tennis court I could feel our bodies reacting to it. Surely you can't deny the pull, it feels like a physical tangible thing' I go on 'Something about you makes me want to keep coming back for more.'

Still indignant she crosses her arms over her chest, poised to tell me something else I don't want to hear. This pushes her delicious plump breasts together and causes her cleavage to raise. I stare at her chest reverently and an erection strains against my shorts. She looks down at my increasing bulge and then back up at me, her blue eyes incredulous but her pupils dilate giving her away.

'Oh' she says

'Do you see what you do to me?' I ask her not sure in my own mind where this is going but I am unable to evade the way my body is reacting to her again.

She appears to shake herself to reason and huffs 'not this again' and turns round to shut the storage bench with the stacked cushions inside.

I take a step towards her and gently take hold of her pony tail. She stills and stands up. I lean towards her, pull the material of her dress aside to give me better access, and plant soft kisses along from the back of her hair line, down her neck and along the ridge of her shoulder. I repeat the same on the other side.

She shivers, but doesn't stop me and goose bumps appear on her arms. She lets out a little moan. This encourages me further and my fingertips stroke up and down the backs of her arms. I continue alternating kisses and strokes.

'I know you want this too, tell me to stop if you really don't' I ask her huskily.

For a moment she is quiet then in a whisper she acquiesces.

'I don't know, I don't know what I want sometimes ...... but at this moment I don't want you to stop'

I can't help a little smile 'Good girl' I say 'turn around, bend forward and put your hands on the bench'

She does what I ask her. The sight of her beautiful round ass in the big knickers does crazy things to my mind and if my erection could have gotten any bigger it does so then. The pressure inside my trousers increases almost unbearably, anymore and I will be seeing stars.
I bend down and carefully remove the panties, as I do so I sink my teeth gently into the smooth white flesh of her bottom and bite down. It causes her back to arch then she moans.

'You like it rough then?' Before she has time to answer my hand swings out and plants a smack on her backside. She screams.

'What the fuck .....?!'

I follow the smack with a massage, she moans and I enjoy seeing her flesh go pinker with the imprint of my palm. I reach to her clit and feel her juices soak my finger.

'Dirty girl' my other hand reaches out and I smack her again. Again she screams but then moans and pants as I massage both her clit and the spot where my palm had met her skin. I deliver three more smacks and follow them up with more massaging. This is so hot, I want to imprint the vision of her marked ass on my brain for evermore.

I cover my finger further in her wetness, circle her clit a few times and then put the finger to her lips.

'Taste my finger, see how good you taste and how wet you are for me' She licks her lips as if anticipating the taste of her own delicious juices.

Her tongue darts out and swipes across my finger then she takes its whole length into her mouth and sucks hard. The sensation of her sucking my finger makes a delicious pulling feeling low in my groin and the sight of her moistened ample lips around my finger is so arousing it makes me want to come all over her ass. I love that she is so absorbed in this moment and as invested in this foreplay as I am, I want this moment to last.

'Lift up your arms' as she does I slide her dress up and over her head. She quivers a little at the loss of her clothing, I massage up her back and when my hands get to her bra strap I undo the clip. Her breasts released, I reach round her and cup them in my hands they feel amazing, so soft I caress them as she straitens up. I turn her slowly around, I haven't actually seen her boobs before and the sight is beyond my imaginings. They are perfection, so soft, full and pert, her nipples pointing up towards me and all totally natural no scars hiding silicon underneath. I stoop down, I could bury my head there and never come up for air. I take one nipple into my mouth and roll my tongue around on it, she moans in appreciation. Then I deliver a little bite, she squeals and stiffens, then relaxes. I release my teeth and watch as it puckers and firms.

To my surprise she says 'My other breast is feeling left out' she twists and offers her other side to me. I am more than happy to oblige.

Now my dick is really complaining

'I need to be inside you'

She looks into my eyes, nods once calmly and I take her lack of objection as consent.

'Turn around again and put your hands on the bench'

She complies as I feel into my pocket and find a condom, thanking God I am always prepared. I hold the packet in my mouth as I drop my shorts and briefs and step out of them. I roll the sheath onto my erection, position myself behind her and slowly enter her glorious glistening pink pussy. The sensation, even through the condom, is liquid gold. One day we will do this with no latex barriers my subconscious registers.

What?

I start to move in and out in slow deliberate movements, she moans appreciatively. Spying a small mirror fixed to the wall behind the bench I can see our bodies move together in its reflection. It is about the most erotic thing I have ever witnessed.

'God you're so beautiful' I say spontaneously out loud.

'Look at yourself in that mirror' she looks towards it and then our eyes catch each other in the reflection. We hold our gaze as

I move in and out, riding her like we are on the road to heaven. I crave more of her so I push deeper and deeper, the sound and feel of my balls slapping against her pussy sends me into orbit.

Her panting and moaning increase and this fuels me on, I fuck her harder and faster. I feel her pussy pulsing round my cock and I can't go on any longer.

'Fuck you're amazing' I say as I ejaculate hard inside her. She screams and bucks and we orgasm together the intense pleasure riding fathomless through my body, I want it to go on and on.

I hold her as the beating of our hearts slows down, wanting to prolong the moment inside her still so soft and warm. We stay connected for a few moments and I quietly try to deal with the conflicting feelings I have towards her.

Reluctantly I pull out and discard the condom in a dustbin. We get dressed without speaking.

I am the first to break the silence.

'That was incredible'

'It was' she concedes 'but we've got to stop whatever this is before it gets out of hand' She stands up, turns her gorgeous naked body to me and looks imploringly at me 'You are a player and I don't want to get my heart broken. I have a good career, which is important to me, I can't afford to lose focus and have my own trauma to cope with. You are used to this, you can deal with it and come out unscathed.' Then she adds 'I might not.'

She pulls on her panties, puts her dress back on in silence and makes her way to the doorway. Turning back to me she says resolutely

'This must end now' and leaves me standing half dressed in the hut. The sun has dropped outside and even though it is summer suddenly it feels rather cold.

CHAPTER 12

Benedict

For the first time in a long time I need to be on my own and think. There is a small drinks fridge in the corner of the hut, I open the door and find a bottle of beer, perfect. There is an opener fixed to a piece of string on top , I hear the satisfying hiss as the bottle opens and take a quick bubbly sip before taking myself outside to sit on one of the un-cushioned chairs.

'Player' is what she called me, and I 'would come out of this unscathed' I hadn't thought that, perhaps until this point, there was even a 'this'. I hadn't felt the need to complicate things. She is a challenge and I am a competitive bastard, I just wanted to wipe that vitriolic expression off her face that she always assumes when she is around me. The opportunity this week had been too good to ignore. I hadn't meant to go back for more after the second time. In my mind I had technically won our little battle and should have left good alone but there is something about her which makes me want more. I must respect her wishes though and stop toying with her.

We are away a lot with the regiment, and I keep myself entertained wanking in the shower reliving one of my many lays I'd had the pleasure of while on leave, or masturbating over the plentiful centrefolds littered around the mess. I don't want to be always pining, agonisingly over a girl friend who is probably messing around behind my back while I am away. While I am in control of my liaisons I won't be made a cuckold of. I will never let that happen again, once was enough, I got my fingers burnt and won't put myself through that torment again.

I was 22, had been to university and then was close to completion of my training at The Royal Military Academy Sandhurst, when I met Charlotte. She had come to one of the college's parties with some friends of hers and she blew my mind. She was beautiful, intelligent and such good fun, unlike anyone I had met before. She was the first person I had met who could match my appetite for sex, her drive as ferocious as mine. We got together that night, one look in her doe-like brown eyes and bonkers dark curls and I was hooked from the word go. We spent every hour we could when I wasn't training with each other. My mates told me we were made for each other and I thought we would always be together pinching myself at my good fortune of meeting the girl of my dreams while I was still young.

The first time I went on commission to Germany I was away for 3 months. We facetimed every day, it was my ritual, and I lived and looked forward to it throughout all the hours I was on exercise or sitting at a desk, preoccupying my thoughts until we saw each other on the screen for that one hour every twenty four.

The days had dragged so slowly, it had been the longest 3 months of my life. Finally we were reunited back in London and the first night I spent at her flat. We were awake most of the night talking and screwing, she had been a little off, but I had just put that down to my recent absence. I had asked a few times if she was ok but she had just brushed me off and I hadn't thought to question it at the time.

The next morning she had woken up before me and was taking a shower when her phone pinged on the bedside table indicating a text. The noise had woken me so without thinking I reached out and grabbed the phone assuming it was mine. Without needing to use the pass code the message was illuminated on the phone's home screen. It was from 'Dave' and said simply

'missed u last night – give me a call when u can'

My heart plummeted, but I still couldn't get my head round her wrong doing. I just couldn't accept it.

She had come out of the shower with a towel round her and seeing me awake she had run towards the bed squealing in delight, as if she was going to jump on me. Then she saw me with her phone in my hand looking stunned, she stopped dead in her tracks as if she had hit a brick wall, the expression on my face telling her what I had unwittingly found out.

First of all she had tried to brush it off as if it was a totally innocent text from a friend. When I was having none of that the tears came, and the apologies, and the promises that I was the one she loved and that she had made a massive mistake.

My heart had shattered, the bubble burst and I couldn't go back. Once that trust had collapsed and that comfortable world of love and hope and excitement for the future I had cocooned myself in had ruptured, my soul was broken. What hurt the most, and still does, is that she had been able to carry on in our relationship without any apparent misgivings and I had been clueless to her deceit.

I left her flat that day and never looked back. I'd had a self-destructive leave week following our split, getting drunk and screwing a different girl every night, but I'd pulled myself together and vowed not the be the victim ever again.

My phone pings in my pocket. Pulling me out of my reverie, there is a text from Claud

'where r u? supper in 15 – cum find me b4 u go down'

I text back a thumbs up emoji, stand up, pull the door too on the tennis hut and make my way back up to the house.

CHAPTER 13

Beatrice

It is the day of the ball and the house is bustling with activity. We are banned from the three front rooms, the hallway, dining room and drawing room, while they are being prepared for later. It is starting to look amazing, I observe the goings on as I cross the main stair case and look down over the bannisters. There is a team of caterers laying up tables and florists artfully arranging flowers as table centres and on pedestals. I eye the other props they are adding to the arrangements, candelabra, books, masks, feathers and even faux animal skulls of something or another, very theatrical, it fuels my excitement for later.

Ursula has arrived and we are going out for a ride this morning with Holly, it keeps us out of the way of the preparations in the house. It is ages since I have been on a horse and I am looking forward to it. I rode a lot when I was younger, I loved eventing and competed in my teens, but busy London life means there is no room for my childhood passion.

Descending the back stairs I make my way through the kitchen and grab a croissant on my way past from the island. A left-over from breakfast which I had missed because I had decided to have a lie-in. I hadn't been in the mood to face the rest of the guests, or one in particular, for obvious reasons.

Also I am a bit sore. I have been wallowing in my post fuck fug all night but feel sated. I woke up with a smile on my face and my fanny was throbbing. Not wanting to miss out on making the most of that added bonus, I kept myself entertained for a while longer, thoughts of a particular ripped body and my bottom being smacked was enough to send me to that happy place again. If I am going to get laid it is infinitely more fun with a hot bastard like Benedict than someone clueless in the art. I have been reconciling with myself. Since my stay at Messina Hall, my libido has taken over from any rational control I had, I might as well have glorious memories than sour regrets and not dwell too harshly as to who it was with.

I just mustn't get attached.
At all.
He is trouble ...... with A CAPITAL T.

Selecting a riding hat which fits me from the tack room at the end of the house, I go outside in search of Holly and Ursula. I find them already at the stables and tacking up their horses when I get there. I say a brisk sing songy 'morning!' as I walk past them and poke my head over the third stable door. Megan, the groom, is in there brushing a horse which I assume is my mount for the morning.

'Hi' I say 'Thank you for getting started on ?' I pause as I don't know the horse's name.

'He's called Gunner. And my pleasure, he loves being groomed, he just needs tacking up now.'

'That's no problem I can take over from here' we smile as I enter the stable and she leaves.

Gunner is a beautiful liver chestnut, quite chunky he looks like an Irish Draught or at least a cross of some sort. He sniffs gently on my gloved hand and then up to my nose, when I walk up to him. I can't resist a kiss on his velvety muzzle. I inhale, enjoying that delicious sweet musky smell, unique to their muzzles, and so resonant from my younger years. I stroke his neck and then put on his saddle and bridle, fiddling with the unfamiliar straps and running my hand under the girth to make sure nothing is pinching him.

I leave Gunner in his stable, having secured the reins behind the stirrup straps and find Ursula to give her a welcome hug. The three of us then lead our horses out and climb on. Lowering myself gently on the saddle I am grateful it is well padded.

We walk out three abreast chatting as we ride our horses along the back track from the stables. The sun shines down on us and the warmth is soothing. The horses are relaxed too, their hooves clip clop rhythmically on the tarmacked road and they are calmed by our non-stop chatter. Presently we make a turn onto a wooded track, an old signpost marked 'Bridleway' points us in the right direction.

Ursula is keen to hear all the gossip, having only just arrived, so we fill her in on our knowledge of Claud's infatuation with Holly and my suspicions to the blossoming romance between John and Conrad, who have been inseparable for the last couple of days. Poor Boris has been wandering around like a lost puppy, his best friend always seems to be elsewhere.

I fidget on my saddle a couple of times, trying to make myself comfortable, Holly is on to me.

'What's wrong Bea, have you got insects in your panties or something? All attention turns to me 'Anyone would think you have just had a good seeing to!'

Oh my God If only they knew how.

I look away and laugh, as if it is a ridiculous thing to say, but then I blush guiltily.

'HELLOOO! Have I missed something?'

'Anything you care to tell us?' Ursula probes.

I try to brush it off and pull my jodhpurs, pretending they are uncomfortable, but Holly is suspicious she knows me too well and I can't hide anything from her.

So I spill all, unable to hold my secret to myself any longer.

I recount my tripping on the hall carpet when we first arrived and what that led to. The spying on him swimming yesterday morning, (including details of his pleasing physique) being caught and what that led to. And finally being introduced to an alternative foreplay in the tennis hut yesterday afternoon and what that led to.

The girls stare at me their mouths agape. They are silent for a few moments, processing my news. Then Ursula asks

'When you say alternative do you mean spanking and stuff?'

They both giggle. I blush even more.

'Oh my God he spanked you?!' Holly incredulously asks 'And you let him?'

'Amazing what you find out about yourself, it was kind of hot' I bow my head, feeling shameful 'Ugh what have I done?'

'I thought you didn't like him, I mean really didn't like him?' Holly looks at me trying to figure out from my expression what I am feeling.

'I don't, in fact I hate him'

'Ok let me get this straight' Ursula processes 'You hate the guy but you have just had a two day sex fest with him? Hmm, he's hot, undoubtedly, I mean super panty dropping god-like hot. I totally get that part. Why the hate?'

'He's just one of those guys who believes he is God's gift to women. That gets to me to start with.' I try to work through my feelings towards him. 'The female race is a game to him, we are his sport, and it goes against everything I have strived to be. I value my independence and achievement both in my career and my personal conduct. I never wanted to be 'that girl' yet another notch in his bedpost. I am not a prude, not by any means, I have just always assumed I would be in total control when it came to my sex life. I had vowed to myself that I wouldn't lose my head in any affair of the heart thus compromising the other areas of my life like the dedication I can give to my work.'

'But you deserve some fun Bea, you are allowed to have both. You technically haven't done anything wrong' Holly tries to console me.

'But not with him!' I agonise 'I saw him in action last year the first time I met him, working the room, the effect he knew he was having on some of the girls. I knew what he is capable of.'

'Do you have feelings for him?' Ursula asks

'Good god no!' I reply a little too hastily. She eyes me suspiciously 'I just can't seem to say no, my body betrays me every time.'

'Don't beat yourself up you are only human' Holly smiles sympathetically.

'That's what I am trying not to do. The two voices in my head are battling it out, one is the berater and the other has whistles and pompoms and is cheerleading me all the way to orgasm!'

'I'm definitely with her' Ursula adds giggling.

We ride out from the shade of the woodland and the grass track splits running all the way around a large agricultural field.

'This is our opportunity for a canter!' Holly, without any protest from us, urges her horse forward and they take off at speed.

Gunner, realising he is being left behind takes a few sideways steps, makes a small buck and gallops off after Holly's horse. I am not in total control but I hang on and relish the liberating sensation of the wind in my face and the power of Gunner's hooves beating on the firm ground. We catch up with Holly and fall into a more rhythmic pace behind her. My horse's panting regulates with his pace as we loll along behind her. I love the feeling of freedom riding at speed gives me, something I hadn't realised how much I had missed until now.

'There is a small ditch into the next field coming up' Holly shouts back to us 'the horses are used to it just hang on!'

Her horse clears it easily and then Gunner shortens his pace to jump it accurately too. I glance back to see Ursula's horse put in a short step then leap in the air all four feet way above the ditch. She yelps as he takes off, is catapulted up and I can see air between her and the saddle but she manages to cling on. Holly and I break into a fit of giggles at Ursula's attempt to regain her dignity. Tears are streaming down my face both from laughing and the wind generated by our speed. It feels so good.

At the end of the next field we slow to a walk and join the road which I recognise leads to the main drive of the house. We let our horses walk the last mile back to give them a chance to cool down. By the main gate there is a smaller gate in the wall, just wide enough for a person or animal but not a vehicle, to pass through. We go through this gate so that the horses can avoid the cattle grid and stony gravel drive. Holly reaches forward on her horse and opens the gate holding it back for us so that we have a clear passage through it.

'We'll wash the horses off when we get back and then if you wouldn't mind giving me a hand to put them out in their paddock that would great.'

'Of course' 'no problem' Ursula and I chime.

I enjoy the ride up to the front of the house. It is an impressive cream stone Georgian building facing the vista of a rolling valley and I feel like I am in the setting of a period novel. As we near the house and the end of our ride, we see Benedict and Claud with Peter admiring his Aston Martin. It is parked on the sweep of gravel in front of the house, Claud is sitting in the driver's seat and appears to be fiddling with the controls. Benedict looks up at us and our eyes lock. He beams at me, giving me one of his glorious megawatt dimpled smiles. I bask in his gaze, enjoying our moment, and not being able to help myself, I smile back.

Coming to my senses a moment later, I drag my eyes away grateful I can pretend to be distracted by my horse, all too aware that he doesn't need any more encouragement.

'Oh my' says Ursula, who hasn't missed a trick 'you are so in trouble!'

'Yup, don't I just know it' I squeak as butterflies erupt in my tummy.

CHAPTER 14

Benedict

Beatrice is not playing fair. After she gave me a firm talking to about no more playdates, how am I supposed to ignore the sight of her in tight jodhpurs and long black boots, astride and in control of a horse? Do I have to suffice myself with committing the rather wonderful sight to my wank bank memory, to be enjoyed during shower time only? If she knew what she was missing out on, how much fun we could have roleplaying rider and naughty horse (or the other way round) would she have been so frigid about our time left here?

I give her my best smile, it's worth a shot and hasn't failed me in the past.

Ever.

The only trouble was.

I got busted.

At the sound of the girls clip clopping their way towards us Claud, not wanting to miss the opportunity to ogle Holly, climbed out of Pete's car (his idea of wank bank material). I was in the middle of my come fuck me grin and enjoying our little moment of eye locking frisson. When Beatrice looked away and I landed back into real time I feel Claud watching me. He has one eyebrow raised, his arms are crossed and he is regarding me with his head on one side for extra dramatic effect.

'In-ter-es-ting' he says slowly like a comedy Poirot 'anything you care to share?'

I shrug my shoulders, and grin goofishly, I don't feel like sharing 'You know me!' Trying to put him off the scent.

'Oh no! You don't get away that lightly. What are you up to Mountant?'

'Who says I am up to anything?' My face a picture of unconvincing innocence.

'I do, I know you and she is most definitely off limits. I am trying to give a good impression to her cousin and I don't need you fucking things up by having your wicked way with her then leaving your dirty mess for us to clear up in your wake!'

Whoops too late

'Not to mention it wouldn't look good if you've screwed around with the Colonel's niece. Have you thought of that?'

Yup I have – still couldn't help myself

'Ok sorry I will try to keep my hands to myself...' I say like a naughty school boy. I add '... From now on' hoping he doesn't catch the irony.

He shakes his head, still not convinced, but he drops the matter.

Thank God

CHAPTER 15

Benedict

Accepting a glass of champagne from a passing tray, I run a finger round my collar to ease the constriction from the bow tie, adjust my mask and take a good swig. The bubbles fizz on my tongue. I swallow and let out a huff of breath, taking with it the anguish my mind has been battling with. The first alcoholic mouthful soothes it way down as I search for clarity on my predicament. I am perplexed that Beatrice has stopped our playtime when we were getting on so well, but even more perplexed at myself that I don't want to stop playing with her. Usually I am more than happy to find another inkwell to dip my quill in. Usually variety is the spice of life, the more the merrier. But since the last couple of days I have done nothing else than crave her soft thighs, ample bosoms and tight pink pussy. Not to mention her company. She is feisty and contentious but good fun and I love the challenge she gives me. Last night I couldn't sleep, I tried to but my dick had other ideas and kept me awake, its persistent erection never gratified, conjuring visions of my red headed temptress.

But she's not mine

And I can't work out why that bothers me so much.

Masked guests are arriving and the hallway is filling up. As they move around it feels like we are on a stage, actors synchronised to a script. The house is festooned with swaths of gold and navy fabric. Decorated tables shimmer in the flickering candlelight, causing shadows which dance in contrast, the effect is dramatic.

A string quartet is playing in the adjoining room, its soft music lending a sophisticated background to the hum of excited conversation.

Pete joins me, shaking me out of my thoughts. He clinks my drink in cheers as our masks nod to each other in acknowledgement. Then Holly appears looking very attractive in a white dress and pearls.

'Ah Holly just the person I wanted to talk to' he motions to her, she smiles sweetly.
'I'm all ears' then acknowledging me 'Hi Benedict' and she walks away with him.

'Who's that?' Boris, with no warning, blasts in my ear excitedly. I turn to him as he gestures his head in the direction a dark skinned girl in a very tight dress 'She's hot!'

'I don't know shall we find out?'

We approach her. I stick out my hand to introduce us.

'Hi I'm Benedict and this is Boris'

'Megan' she takes my hand and we hug, 'Hi' she says to Boris as they greet. 'I run the stables here. You were part of the advance party weren't you?' She says only to him. I am suddenly the spare part.

'Excuse me' I leave them to it.

I take a few more steps, Ursula is flirting playfully with Tony.

'I recognise the handsome man behind the mask'

'Maybe you are mistaken?' he counters 'Who could I be?'

'None other than the distinguished Sir Anthony, who has the wit and charm I would recognise anywhere!'

A streak of red in my periphery vision catches my attention. My intuition piqued, it recognises, before I do, my new favourite colour. My legs spontaneously move in that direction, jostling around guests as I try to get closer. Her hour-glass figure is shown off to its full glory. Porcelain shoulder blades sit above a snugly fitted strapless dress. Laces crisscrossed up the back pull in at her tiny waist and curve over her gorgeous ass like a 1950's pin up. The feathers of her mask fan out either side of her head and her auburn hair falls in soft waves down her spine.

She slows down to collect a glass of champagne from a passing tray. As the tray moves away she stands casting her eyes around the room and takes a sip. There are conversations and guests all around us and I take my opportunity.

Standing behind her I whisper into her ear, my voice deep and low, so only she can hear.

'I'm looking for somebody called Beatrice. Have you seen her?'

I enjoy the effect I have on her. Goosebumps appear down her arm, she shivers a little and I can feel her smiling. Warmth radiates back to me and makes me involuntarily smile too.

She doesn't turn around but continues our little game.

'Will you not tell me who you are?'

'Not now' I say

'I will keep a look out for your Beatrice – tell me about her?'

'She is very beautiful.'

She takes a sharp intake of breath and I continue.

'Be careful though she can be fiery if you fly too close you will burn your wings – mine are a little singed.'

I run my nail lightly across the top of her shoulder, imagining her nipples hardening and her pussy coming to life.

'She is beguiling, an enchantress, just watch out that she doesn't steel your heart.'

I am still close to her ear and see her lick her lips and then bite on her bottom lip. She is thinking and slowly breaths in and out.

Wait a minute. What's that – whoa! Can it be? Oh yes .... Her hand has landed on my crotch and has cupped my man parts.

Oh yes ... yes ...YES!

She squeezes gently and her fingers drum lightly on my balls. I let out a groan.

'Tell me more about her?' Her fingers continue their gentle massage.

I try to concentrate on saying something clever but I struggle against the sensation of her touch, it is overriding my thinking.

'I don't think she likes my friend.' My voice goes higher at the end of my sentence. 'He doesn't understand why'

'What do you think?'

'I think he wants to spend more time with her but she always seems very grumpy with him.'

The nails dig in and squeeze. I wince my eyes watering.

'I have an idea' I say. She releases her grasp on my balls and drops her hand. I let out the breath I was holding in.

Running my fingers down the length of her left arm, over her hand, I lace our fingers together. The connection reignites the spark I feel when we touch, the familiar pull, an invisible power that draws me to her.

'Come with me.'

Working our way through the crowded rooms I pull her away from the main throng of guests. Sometimes she has to break into a little jog to keep up with me. Off to the side of the drawing room there is another corridor which leads to rooms at the back of the house. I reach out for the door knob, casting my eye around the room one last time to make sure we are not being noticed. I pull her through and spin her round so her back is against the wall. The hallway is deserted of guests and dimly lit by a couple of pearlescent wall lights. Reprieve at the sudden quiet enveloping us, the door bangs closed, I can hear the sound of her quickened breathing and it makes my dick stir in anticipation.

She looks deep into my eyes, searching for something. Is she starting to resign herself to the chemistry that is undeniably between us? She draws her lower lip into her mouth and slowly releases it, glistening wet. I lower my face closer and my lips gently brushes hers, the sensation is dynamite. I raise my head one more time to drink in her gorgeous face before I go in for the killer kiss.

CLANG!
CLANG!
CLANG!

Ugh it's the gong calling everyone to sit down for dinner. Certainly not saved by the bell, more like death by blue balls.

'Bloody hell' I groan 'couldn't have been worse timing'

Beatrice giggles at me as reluctantly we compose ourselves, standing apart and straightening our masks. Running my hands through my hair I take a resigned breath, open the door and we scoot through like wayward children. Beatrice overtakes me and impressively negotiates the guests heading towards their tables to look at the table plan which is propped on an easel at the bottom of the main staircase. She turns round and we nearly bump into each other.

'We're both on table 2, it's just behind you.' She points to our allotted seating, we find our name places and wait by the chairs for the others on our table to join us.

John, Boris, Conrad, Claud and Ursula are all on our table, along with Megan and a couple of other girls who are local friends of Holly's. As one of the ball's hostesses Holly is sitting on the 'top table' with her parents, Beatrice's father Tony, Major Peter and some other older, presumably family friends.

Claud's disappointment at her not sitting at our table is palpable and he looks forlornly towards her. Us men busy ourselves with pouring wine, I have Megan on my right and a Sophie on my left. She's very pretty, blond, big boobs and a captivating smile. Just my type and normally I would be all over her but my attention is always across the table at a certain red head. I know she is also keeping an eye on me. Megan is turned and chatting animatedly to Boris so I immerse myself in finding all there is to know about Sophie. No harm in provoking the green eyed monster if it creates a little competition from the other side of the table.

We are tucking into a delicious smoked salmon mousse when John, who is the other side of Sophie, announces rather loudly

'Looks like my brother is getting on very well with Holly'

Well that's not helpful, the dickhead. Claud's eyes shoot to Holly and he looks between her and Pete. His shoulders slump and he takes a rather too large mouthful of his wine. I try to brush it off knowing what Pete is up to.

'He's an old family friend and hasn't seen her for months, probably lots of catching up to do'

'She's punching above her weight with him anyway' John says. I don't know what his problem is. He is a devious cunt, I am worried he might be up to something.

'If your brother could ever be so lucky I would say it would be the other way round.' Claud slurs.

The meal continues and I observe Claud doesn't engage with

anyone just keeps drinking. After the pudding we are served with cheese and coffee. Leo stands up and delivers a speech about the Help for Hero's charity and the worthwhile projects it is working on. I am worried about Claud he is swaying in his seat, Holly keeps looking across at our table, concern showing on her face too.

When Leo sits down and everybody claps Claud stands up.

'Excuse me' he says

As he swerves to get round a seated guest he pitches to the side. I leap out of my chair to catch him.

'Ok there buddy'

He tries to push me away

'I'm fine'

'Let's just make our way out of here'

He allows me to prop him up as we go through the back to find the bathroom.

On the way he is muttering and swearing, leaning heavily on me.

'Fucking Pete, what's he up to?' he slurs 'Told me he would put a good word in for me but I think that was ruse to trick me. Look at him all over Holly like that, rubbing it in my face'

'It's not what you think' I try to reason with him, hopeless as he has drunk so much.

'I said leave me alone!' he pulls away from me and then reels to the side. I grab him again to stop him falling. He swings round and with a surprisingly weighty left hook punches me on my jaw. Caught off guard I get spun round and I clutch my face, it bloody hurts. There is a metallic taste in my mouth, blood, I must have bitten my tongue.

Claud takes one look at me unapologetically and staggers into the bathroom.

Standing in the middle of the room I take my mask off and hold my face, Pete walks in.

'Good God what's going on?'

'Just been on the receiving end of one of Claud's finest uppercuts' I wiggle my jaw as the blood returns and the pain starts to register fully.

'What? Why?'

'He thinks you are cracking onto Holly for yourself and didn't like it when I tried to reason him out of it'

'Oh bloody hell what a mess'

Beatrice appears.

'What is going on? Where's Claud' then looking at me 'Oh my God what's happened to your face?'

'Claud punched him' says Pete 'And I think I am partially to blame'

'It looks sore' she says taking a closer look 'I'm going to get some ice.'

Holly joins us too, as Beatrice goes to the kitchen, she is looking around us.

'Where's Claud?' then looking at me 'Oh what happened?'

'Don't worry, a misunderstanding, no harm done'

'Is Claud ok?'

'He will be, after a few glasses of water and some reassurance from you.' Pete interjects

'Oh why? She looks confused

'He thought I was flirting with you.'

'Eeew' Holly blushes a little and laughs 'I mean, no offence, but we have known each other for a very long time.'

'Why don't you tell Claud that' my friend comes out of the bathroom looking rather pale.

Beatrice reappears with ice and holds it to my jaw. She has taken off her mask and I enjoy watching her and soaking up the comfort it gives me.

'Go on give him a hug or something' she encourages Holly.

Holly runs to Claud and flings her arms around him.

'You are such a wally!' she says then plants a smacking kiss on his lips. He looks shocked and his eyes widen at all of us, then his hands go to back of her neck and their kiss turns into an all-out snog.

'At bloody last!' says Beatrice to them 'now get a room please'

None of us want to continue witnessing the snog fest so we leave them to it. Pete returns to the dining hall.

'Come to the kitchen, I think you need to sit down for a few minutes.' Beatrice takes my arm which is holding the ice to my face and guides me through. I am quite enjoying the attention from nursey caring Beatrice, its novel to see her like this and I play bruised and battered patient for a little longer.

I sit down at a chair next to the table as she fusses round me, stroking the hair out of my eyes and pulling the ice away from my face to inspect the bruise.

'It's blossoming nicely. I wonder if there is some arnica somewhere in here.'

A passing waitress overhears 'there's a medicine drawer in the end dresser' pointing at the facing wall 'try that.'

She goes to the dresser, opens the drawer and rummages inside.

'Ah – here we go, perfect'

She walks back, pulls out the adjoining chair to mine and sits down opposite me. Slowly she lowers my arm, opens the cap of the arnica tube and squeezes a small amount onto her finger.

'Is this ok?' She asks my permission before she applies the cream.

'Of course'

She delicately rubs the cream onto the bruised area, leaning towards me I have the bird's eye view of her cleavage. That and with her close proximity I can smell her perfume, my senses are awakened and I can feel stirrings down below.

Not now - control yourself Benedict.

Her hand stills from its administrations and hovers near my face. I reach up and take hold of her wrist, angling my face towards it I plant whisper soft kisses up and down her forearm.

She whimpers in appreciation.

Our tender moment is interrupted by the band starting to play, Beatrice stands up.

'Come on, if you are ok, I feel like dancing.'

CHAPTER 16

Beatrice

I take his hand and pull him back to the main hallway, where the tables have now been cleared back. The band, who are on a low platform in front of the main door, are midway through their first song. It's a pretty good version of the Beatles classic 'Twist and Shout'. My aunt and uncle have led the dancing and are performing a very slick rock n roll. More and more guests are piling onto the dance floor and I wonder what sort of dancer Benedict is. Not all men I have met enjoy dancing, some prefer spending the evening by the bar and interacting that way. I can spend all night on the dance floor, especially if the music is good. I am yet to meet a man who shares my appetite. I am kind of hoping Benedict is not one, I don't need any more points on the positive list.

The scales balance once again in his favour .....

As we step onto the chequered floor Benedict is ahead of me. He reaches out a hand, grabs mine and spins me in towards him, I spiral along the length of his arm and end up with my back is to his chest.

Oh wow

I am flung out again, he lifts his arm up and I turn in a circle under it. Then he lifts my arms up and out, my left arm goes over itself and behind my ear, he pulls away from my outstretched right arm and slides apart. As I think I am going to stumble into the others, my hand is expertly grasped and I am spinning once again into him. We continue to dance with me getting used to following his moves and just about managing to keep up.

Drawing attention to ourselves the others start to form a circle around us. I am spun, flung out and twisted time and again, really enjoying myself and the attention we are garnering. He is a god on the dance floor, and as the song draws to a close, my cheeks are red and I cannot stop smiling and laughing. I am finally pulled in to his chest as the others applaud us. Benedict bows, quite at home performing to a crowd.

The next song performed is Mr Brightside by the Killers, one of my favourites. It is a rock but not a roll number so we face each other less formally. Always popular, it feels like most of the guests are piling onto the dance floor and we are pushed together. He puts his hand around me, to the small of my back, and holds me closer as he grinds his hips towards mine and we move in time to the music. As the song progresses and the music is more upbeat I jump round and grind my backside into his moving hips. It is really hot... he is really hot and we move in tune, his front to my back as he has one arm around me holding my middle, the other in the air. I think he becomes affected by our position a little as he turns me round and we finish the dance face to face.

He shows no signs of wanting to give up so we wait for the next performance, the band roll on into 'It must have been love' by Roxette. A slower song, Benedict holds me close, his face is near mine and he bends his head lower and whispers in my ear.

'We dance well together, shows how compatible our bodies instinctively know they are.'

That commanding voice and suggestive tone does things to my insides, but I want to enjoy our time so I laugh a little to brush it off. I snuggle into his chest and inhale that unique manly scent he has, laying my head on him. He in turn puts his head above mine, it feels intimate, without the onus of impending passion and I want to savour the moment. We stay locked in this way for the rest of the dance, feeling surprisingly at home in his hold but reminding myself how temporary our connection will inevitably be.

As the song comes to an end we reluctantly pull apart. He looks affectionately towards me, just for a second and then suggests we should go and get a drink. I feel he has had the same talk to himself about the boundaries of our liaison as I have made a point of reminding him previously.

We head away from the dance floor towards the bar which has been set up at the edge of the drawing room.

CHAPTER 17

Benedict

I lead the way to the bar with Beatrice following me. I am feeling a little off kilter. The intimacy of that last dance and the comfort I enjoyed holding her in my arms is messing with my head. I need a distraction.

John and Conrad are at the bar and are overtly flirting with each other. I didn't know Conrad was gay. It must have been tough being in the army and not feeling like he could be open about his sexuality. I am pleased he has come out by default, being here with his three closest colleagues. We are able to support him, if he needs it, when we are back with the regiment. News like this will travel, despite the fact that I don't think either of the three of us would be indiscrete. His closest friend is Boris who, looking like he might hook up with Megan, won't feel so much like the third wheel for the rest of the weekend. It will keep him distracted if they continue a relationship and give him something else to focus on.

'Would you like a drink?' I turn to Beatrice

'I need something soft, I'm thirsty from dancing, elderflower or sparking water, or whatever they have please'

I gesture to the bartender and order for the two of us. Leaning on the bar while I wait for the drinks, I overhear John saying something to Conrad.

'Are you sure they kissed?'

Conrad replies 'Definitely your brother told me.'

Our drinks arrive so I miss the next bit of their conversation. I give the bartender some money 'Keep the change' I nod as I take both drinks.

'.....And now Boris is eating the groom?' John questions

Conrad laughs, 'That's one way to put it!'

Turning round I see John give Conrad a kiss and then he sends him off. For a fleeting moment it concerns me, I don't trust John and hope his intensions to my colleague are honourable. I don't have time to dwell on this though because I have a sexy red head to entertain and want to keep her attention.

'Are you staying here beyond the weekend? I ask her, I have to shout a bit as the band are playing a rowdier song. She moves her head closer to hear.'

'Sadly not. We have a big case coming up so I've got to be back in the office on Monday. I'm going to leave after brunch on Sunday, at least we have tomorrow to relax.' She smiles then puts her head on one side 'Why do you ask, what are your plans?'

'We have next week off too. I was wondering .....'

Boris comes jostling past us 'Howz it going?' he interrupts

'All good mate' I reply 'You?'

He grins 'Just enjoying all that hot Megan has to offer!'

I roll my eyebrows.

'Anyway I've been summoned by John so I'll leave you two love birds to it'

'We're not love birds' Beatrice interjects

'Yeah whatever' Boris winks at me and moves off to join John at the bar.

'It's too hectic in here' I observe 'let's find somewhere quieter'

Beatrice finishes her drink and handing me the empty glass says 'I know somewhere, follow me'

I return the empties to the bar and follow her back through the different rooms, past the dancing and back out to the kitchen then onto the utility room, it's much quieter out here which is calmer. I pause, taking a moment to take a breath, spying a drinks fridge in the corner housing some spare champagne I help myself to a bottle, grab a couple of glasses and a bowl of left over strawberries I see sitting on the worktop. I catch up with Beatrice and follow her down another corridor.

CHAPTER 18

Beatrice

I open the door to the tack room and reach for the light. There are a number of switches so I try one, it illuminates a wall light which casts just enough yellowish glow to see clearly but is not all out dazzling. Bridles line the wall, hanging on hooks and beyond them racks housing the many saddles which must have accumulated over the years. There is a bench running round two sides of the room, a sink with tack cleaning equipment sitting on some shelves next to it along with riding hats and other clothing. I suddenly feel a little apprehensive, it is very quiet, just the two of us, a tension in the air.

Benedict puts down a bowl of strawberries on the bench.

'Hold these' he says handing me the flutes.

He tears the foil from the top of the champagne bottle and gently twists out the cork. The bottle hisses and he holds it over the glasses as the pale liquid pours into each one. Handing me a glass he clinks his against mine.

'Cheers' he says with his deep voice and we take a sip, not taking his eyes from mine, then he leans forward and gently kisses me. I liquefy at his contact, my whole body tingling, we continue exploring with our tongues colliding in slow seductive discovery, the remnants of the champagne enhancing our chemistry, making me feel connected in a way I have never before.

He pulls away, his eyes bore into mine

'Do you trust me?'

I think for a second 'Yes .... Yes at this moment I do – don't ask me the same question tomorrow'

He smiles and my core clenches. *Yup my reaction too*! I say to myself. He is a beautiful devil.

He searches around the room and going to the shelves finds a scarf which he pulls out, one of those silk type square ones. Then selects another couple of items, I think they are also scarves or something similar.

He takes another swig of his champagne.

'I'm going to tie this scarf around your head like a blind fold, it will enhance your sensations as you won't be able to see. You must tell me, at any stage, if you want me to stop. Do you understand?

I nod my assent

'I will be gentle, to start with, unless you don't want me to, I promise.' As an afterthought he moves to the door and turns the key in the lock. 'Just to make sure we aren't interrupted.'

Folding the silk scarf he rolls it down to a blind fold shape then stands behind me reaching over my head and covers my eyes. I wipe my wayward hair out of the way and adjust the scarf so it sits comfortably. Taking the glass from my hand he moves away. Then I feel him closer again.

'Take a bite. It's the strawberry, then hold it in your mouth and take a sip of the champagne I will give you'

I do as I am told and enjoy the sweetness of the strawberry, I take a gulp from the glass as it touches my lips, and the combination of fizz and acidity is delicious. His finger slowly traces along my lip wiping away the excess liquid, I dart my tongue out to lick the champagne from it then suck his whole finger into my mouth. He groans and it makes me shiver, I have never felt more responsive and I want more.

Benedict start to kiss down my neck, then he turns me around lifts my hair to the side and kisses across the back of my shoulders. All I can do in response is sigh, my skin is tingling feeling like it is being caressed by a million feathers, each kiss amazing, the sensation like cold fire to my skin.

I feel him undoing the laces on my dress, the pull and tug and brush of his fingers causing cart wheels inside me. My dress drops and I hear him exhale. I am wearing red lace panties and hold up stockings.

'You're fucking perfect' he exclaims, then stands still for a few moments as if admiring the view 'take my hand and step out from your dress.'

As I step out he pulls the dress away. His other hand caresses my nipple, causing it to harden, becoming hyper aware and reacting to the air current as he moves around me. I feel his hot mouth on my breast and his tongue dances on the nipple finished with his teeth drawing gently back. He repeats on my other breast. All sensation is centred on my chest as it feels alive, swollen and full and a ball of desire starts to build low in my belly.

'More' I breathe

He takes one hand and I feel soft fabric being wrapped and bound around my wrist, he pulls tight.

'Is that ok, not too tight?' It feels snug but not restricting

'It's good' I all but pant in reply

Then he takes my other hand and attaches another soft scarf, and pulls to the same tautness.

'I'm going to suspend your arms from the bridle hooks – if you feel uncomfortable tell me.'

Oh my God can this get any hotter? I throb deliciously at the thrill of being tied up and my heartbeat forcibly thumps in my chest.

'Ok' I say in a gush of breath

First one arm gets lifted up, a bridle jingles as it is removed from the hook and the scarf tied around in its place, after a few tugs I can move my wrist and hands but they remain suspended. My other arm has the same treatment so I am now restrained with my hands shackled to the hooks either side of my head. This makes my chest prouder than the rest of my body, I can feel my biceps taught.

Without warning he takes hold of both nipples squeezes and twists. I scream. The pain suddenly excruciating.

'What the fuck are you doing? .... Oh'

As blood returns to my breasts an intense pleasure shoots to my pussy. I come and moisture pools between my legs.

He puts his hand down my panties and feels inside me, his finger exploring, my clit swollen and screaming for release. I grind my hips forward trying to get some friction from his touch.

'I knew you would be wet for me – your delicious pussy wants more doesn't it?'

I whimper. I do want more.

He grabs my nipples again and twists. Again I scream. The paid sudden, it stings like hell, then light shoots up my spine and I orgasm, my body bucking as he maintains his hold on my breasts. He releases. I want to touch myself to ride out my orgasm but the restriction of my cuffs prevents me and leaves me feeling fretful.

To my frustration he walks away from me, his footsteps sound across the floor and I hear the jangle of something. It sounds like he has selected a piece of equipment. There is a familiar smacking sound, a riding crop, he is testing it. His movements feel measured and deliberate.

'Are you going to hit me?' I don't know if the thought scares me or excites me and that alone triggers a voltage reaction in my tummy.

'Not yet'

He strokes the soft looped end of the whip around the top laced edge of my stocking on my thigh, it tickles a little and he continues this torture all over my torso. Again I can't stop him as I am bound and this restriction turns from frustration to utter arousal. I throw my head back and exhale a noisy breath, I want to cry out, fling my arms around him and be fucked till Christmas. My arms pull against their bindings and I hear him snigger.

'Patience!' he orders and I still, anticipating his next move.

He holds my panties on either side and guides them down my legs, I step out without being asked.

'Put one leg up on the bench'

I do as I am told and he guides my foot to a firm position. I feel so exposed, my arms held back, breasts pushed forward and now my wet cunt is unveiled by my raised leg.

He stands up slowly pushing the harder end of the crop firmly into my skin and draws it on a path all the way up the inside of my leg and thigh and presses it to my clitoris. Then he moves it around in circles, there is pressure but it is not painful. I close my eyes inside my blindfold and throw my head back as I ride the crop, eliciting an involuntary shudder, that delicious tightening enlivening my senses as I push against the whip my need for release desperate. He drags the crop up between my folds, the plaited leather reverberates against my clit as he pulls the whole length through, each ridge of the leather bumping through in a jackhammer rhythm. I moan in pleasure, it feels like it will never stop and I want to fly, the sensation is so intense.

'Oh my God that feels amazing'

I feel him smile in satisfaction.

'You are so wet for me, but I can make you even wetter. I'm going to make your pussy cry out in its need for me'

Smack, the whip stings against the side of my butt.

Ow!

'Fuck!'

My first feeling is total anger, I yelp incensed, then humiliation at the power he has, in this moment, over me. I start to pant. He massages where the whip smarted me. A depraved confusing combination of fury, disgust, pulsating pussy and an overwhelming need for more of the same, I didn't know I could feel. My fetish I hadn't realised I had, craves insatiably further torture.

What?

'Again!' I stammer

'You are such a dirty girl'

Thwack, thwack.

More massage. My juice trickles down my thigh.

'Jesus that is one hot centrefold' he exhales heavily, feeling with his hand that his mind is not deceiving him.

Thwack, Thwack. Massage

'Oh God yes'

'I am marking you, these red lines I own, do you know that?'

Thwack, thwack.

'Yes I do'

Massage

'That creamy white ass belongs to me, your orgasm is mine, every wave of pleasure and every shudder. I'm going to fuck you so hard nothing and nobody will compare to this.

'Jesus Christ'

'Don't give him the credit. I want my name screamed when you orgasm.'

I hear the rip of a packet. He is putting a condom on.

He holds my hips and slowly inserts his cock inside me. It is so hard and erect it fills me, its girth tight against my walls. Wondering if I can take any more he starts to move in and out.

My blindfold is removed without warning, although the light is dim the sudden shock of brightness make me squint for a second.

'Open your eyes and look at me' he demands 'I want to see you when you orgasm'

His movements are steady and controlled in and out as he maintains a smooth rhythm, my need for release is driving me crazy and I want more, more speed, more depth, more friction.

I look into his eyes, wildly imploring him to give me what I need and emit a mewling growl of frustration.

'Only when I say' he orders in response

Offering my mouth for a kiss, I lick along his lip line, suck his lower lip into my mouth and bit hard. Relishing the chance to return the torture.

He hisses and pulls back 'Fuck you' he grabs the whip and delivers a sharp smack to my thigh.

The furnace inside me detonates as molten heat sears from the sting to my core, I scream and it drives me on. He gives in and pushes harder and faster his momentum increasing.

'Yes, yes, don't stop!'

'Look at me' he bellows as he pounds into me and I meet every one of his thrusts. Crying out he comes and roars, the sound primordial.

'Benedict!' I scream in response as I orgasm so intensely my insides gripping and milking and throbbing. The sensation goes on and on as we stare into each other eyes spellbound.

'You are a fucking Goddess' he reverently says to me. We stay attached neither one able to withdraw from the magnitude of the moment. His hands are on the wall behind my shoulders, next to my shackled arms, he leans his head closer resting his forehead on mine and closes his eyes. I can hear his breathing slow, we are both lost in our own minds, although I cannot form the words in my head which explain the weight of emotion I am feeling. Whatever it is I try to shut out as an incredible sensation of post coital calm filters through my whole body.

Eventually he pulls out. Untying my hands from the hooks he says,

'I want to sleep with you tonight. I want to lie next to you' he reinforces his request with a gentle kiss to my lips. It is surprisingly tender and affectionate.

This is unexpected, I am temporarily seduced by the idea but not sure. Spending the night together muddies the lines drawn in my mind. I had agreed with myself that I could have some fun but I need to be able to walk away with my feelings intact and no regrets. He continues to kiss me, gentle kisses to my mouth, along my jawline and down my neck. I want to give in, submit to his sentiment, but I absolutely don't believe this is anything more to him than a weekend activity. I can't be like this, switching my feelings on and off and I can't get attached.

'I don't know' he looks up surprised that I have reacted like this 'I don't think it is a good idea.' I try to quantify 'I need to go back to my life next week with a clear conscience, able to re-focus and not harbouring an attachment to you.'

He looks deeper into my eyes and stares. I can almost see the thoughts churning around in his head.

'Ok' he looks kind of despondent 'I understand'

I find my dress, step into it and pull it up.

'You'll have to help me with this' I turn my back to him and he obliges retying the laces.

'Would you like to walk back separately so as not to raise suspicion if we are seen together?' he offers

'Thank you yes that's a good idea, give me five minutes' I have made up my mind but there is a nagging feeling, like a tempting angel, or devil, arguing with my resolve, that perhaps just one night won't do any harm?

Come on Bea, pull yourself together and go

I unlock the door and peer out, it's quiet and looks like the coast is clear. Taking off my shoes I run on tip toes out through the utility room and kitchen to the back stairs which lead up to my bedroom.

What I don't see is Claud and Holly, hidden in their own tryst under the staircase. But they see me and five minutes later they see Benedict too.

CHAPTER 19

Benedict

I toss and turn and can't get to sleep after my epic showdown with Beatrice in the tack room. Confusing thoughts buzz in my head, feelings resurface that I have to give conflicting arguments to, so that I don't have to accept the implications of them. I am relieved when the sun comes up and I can get out of bed. I put on my running shorts, top and trainers, grab my phone and ear pods and tread as quietly as possible through the slumbering house. Needing to be on my own, I avoid the main rooms and the risk of bumping into someone, and exit out through the French doors in the orangery. I negotiate the parterre and gardens beyond the swimming pool, walk past the tennis court and climb over a stile which lands me straight onto a footpath. I don't know where it will take me, but I decide to follow it as far as possible.

It's a beautiful morning, the dew is still damp on the ground and the rising sun is casting a rosy glow on the horizon as it commences its climb upwards in the sky. The sound of birds singing, something I never hear in London, makes me feel cheerful. Their delighted energy at the new day rubs off on me as I take a deep breath of fresh morning air and break into a jog.

Running is my best therapy, after five minutes or so my pace and breathing level out and I can keep going for miles. I go to my inner space, my body feels like it is working on autopilot and my mind has the uninterrupted opportunity to try to sort things out. If I have a few days of no running I become irritable and restless, my muscles stiffen and I can't think clearly.

Selecting a play list on my phone, I insert the ear pods, press play and hit the trail finding my rhythm.

My mind immediately goes to thoughts of Beatrice, she was right, of course, I was getting too carried away.

What was I thinking?

I have been made a fool of in the past and vowed to myself I would never let this happen again. Relationships are not for me. I am really happy for Claud that he has finally gotten together with Holly and I have no doubt that it won't be long before they make boyfriend/girlfriend status. They are relationship material and I know they will be happy.

I am not relationship material, I don't have the tolerance for it because I enjoy my freedom too much. I can go abroad for work with a clear conscience that I am not leaving behind a girlfriend, wife or God forbid a child, waiting every hour of every day for my return. I only have to worry about myself financially and am never short of offers for sex when I am on leave so why complicate my life at all?

My time with Beatrice last night blew my mind (and my balls). She is so hot, like super siren hot and I think she discovered a little more about her sexual tastes outside the scope of vanilla lovemaking. Our session in the saddle room was a hard one to beat, I had a hard on the size of the Eiffel tower while I was playing with her. Good job she was blind folded and couldn't see that I was as into it as she was.

I have to respect her wishes and leave our time together as a memory of this weekend. It really pains me though it feels as if we have unfinished business like there is so much more for me to discover about her delicious body and her challenging mind. There's definitely more to her, I have figuratively and literally just touched the surface. She had the good sense to stop me going soppy on her, and what was I thinking wanting to sleep next to her for the night? I just wanted to feel her skin next to mine, smell her gorgeous scent for a bit longer then wake up next to her and, if I would be so lucky, make sweet morning glorious tender love to her.

Anyway I am happy with bachelor life and wish to continue to be single, I never imagine I will change my mind on this. Beatrice has an impressive career and that is the most important aspect of her life. We can both be adult and go our separate ways tomorrow. Normally I want nothing more than this, no strings amazing sex and no repercussions. Not sure what's wrong with me this time, I just can't help myself going back for more, AND more again.

I have been running for 45 minutes or so and covered 7.4 miles according to my running tracker app. My footpath came to a junction and I was able to head back towards the house on a different path. It has brought me round to the road which leads to the front drive. As I leave the track and hit the road my leg muscles object to the harder surface, but I like the pain, my body registers it is working hard and the endorphins keep me on my running high.

Life when I get back to London will be busy for the next week, packing and sorting stuff out. We are being stationed in Herefordshire, but I will have most of my weekends free after the initial settling in period. Maybe I could meet Beatrice for a drink when we are back in London? Just friends. I will see what she thinks, I mean where's the harm in that? Or am I kidding myself?

Slowing to a walk just in front of the house, I stop by a low wall and stretch out my hips, quads and hamstrings. Enjoying pushing into my stretches to gain maximum benefit as my heartbeat returns to normal. I spy a garden tap and taking the chance to quench my thirst, I turn it on and drink a few long sips direct from the faucet. Sticking my head underneath the running water, I thoroughly wet my hair and face to help me cool down. I smooth my hair away from my eyes with both hands as I stand up and turn to enjoy the vista from the side of the house.

Someone else must be up, as I cast my eyes around I can hear women's voices chattering. I look around wondering where the sound is coming from. Still not in a sociable mood, plus I am sweaty and in need of a shower, I try to work out how I am going to get back into the house without being seen.

I decide on a longer route to the orangery and take a detour doubling back up to the tennis court. The sound of conversation is getting louder, it must be coming from the box hedge maze but I still can't actually see anyone. The hedging stands at just under six foot, if I skulk past, head bent I won't be spotted but also won't look suspicious, like I am trying not to be seen, if someone notices me.

As I walk between the court and where the maze border starts, I catch one word of the conversation.

'Beatrice'

My ears prick up and I slow down to see if I can catch more. Straining my head towards the hedge I move a little backwards and forwards to try to hear more clearly. I recognise the voices of Holly and Ursula. Holly is speaking.

'.. was instrumental in getting us together. Oh my God he is so gorgeous, so caring, I really like him. He is such a good kisser too'

Eeeeew

'we have this amazing chemistry it took all my resolve to leave him and go to bed on my own last night'

'I am so happy for you' Ursula says 'he is really lucky to find you. Are you going to meet up in London?'

'Yes definitely, he has a week off still to go but is talking about coming to see me as soon as we get back to London, like tomorrow night!' Holly squeaks in excitement.

'That's so brilliant'

They go quiet for a moment and I shuffle a little to get closer still. The hedge is sticking into the side of my face but I don't care I am compelled to keep listening.

'I hope Bea is ok. Do you think there is something up with her?' Ursula asks

'There is definitely something up with her...' I stick my head further into the bushes desperate not to miss a word. The hedge rustles a bit and Holly stops talking. I freeze trying to ignore the twig working its way in my ear.

'... I know she has feelings for Benedict.' She says quite clearly.

What?!

Butterflies explode in my stomach. I don't believe it, she must have gotten it wrong about her friend.

'..... she just doesn't acknowledge it'

'But how do you know?' Ursula questions

My heart has started to beat faster, I am not sure I want to hear anymore, but the hedge has me impaled in its branches, if I leave now I will give myself away. Truthfully though I wouldn't walk away even if I could.

'He totally gets to her, and she can't accept it so she puts up this big front about her career and that being the most important thing in her life. But deep down I know her.'

'Has she said anything to him?

'Good God no, in fact the opposite, she stomps around as if he were the last man on the planet she would ever consider boyfriend worthy. And gets really cross if you try to question her on it'.

That sounds just like Beatrice, so stubborn, but I kind of like that about her.

'Do you think she would ever change her mind and give in to her feelings?'

'I think she has gone so far in her charade of not liking him she has become her own worst enemy and won't go back on her word. But I think that is making her sad too'

'I wonder if someone told Benedict or he found out somehow and could do something about it.'

'The trouble is he might take the news the wrong way and either use it to his advantage to torment her or maybe run a mile. He does have the reputation of a bit of a playboy – different girl every night when he is on leave and all that.'

Not exactly every night...

'So Bea has a point then, in being cautious'

'Yup she's not stupid. It's a shame though I think Pete likes her too. They would make a good couple'

Something about Holly's last sentence makes me want to smash Pete's face in. The thought of her with anyone else and I suddenly discover a possessiveness I didn't think I had?

'Anyway she would be mortified if she knew we were having this conversation. Don't say anything and especially not a word to Benedict. If it is meant to be it will happen and we must just leave it up to them.'

I experience a rush of unimaginable joy. Why am I reacting like this?

'Let's go back to the house, I think breakfast will be nearly ready.' Ursula says.

I hear them moving away. They are giggling. Hmmm? I duck back round to the back of the maze and plonk myself down on the grass, my head in my hands, trying to absorb their conversation.

I can't believe what I have just heard. It can't be true can it? It has come straight from her cousin and best friend's mouth so it must be real. Beatrice has feelings for me?! Everything Holly said adds up, her belligerence, talk of her career being paramount to her and the apparent front she gives to the world and in doing so denying her honest feelings.

But how do I feel at this news? I would've thought that I would run a mile as Holly said I might. The last time I was in love I was made a fool of, I vowed never again and I have made it my mantra ever since. I will be in for so much abuse from my mates, it pisses me off that they might be proved right. Can I change? Or have I changed already? I assumed, resolutely, that I could be happy on my own, I just didn't believe that I would ever meet anyone who would alter that.

Strangely the thought of Beatrice in my life doesn't terrify me. She is independent, which I like, and doesn't appear to need constant encouragement. She knows her own mind but is caring, you know where you stand with her, and my instinct tells me she is genuine. She is not nagging or needy or doesn't appear to be. Waking up to her every morning would be amazing, the thought of doing so gives me an excited buzz, now I come to terms with the idea I don't want to think of it not happening at all.

I stand up with a renewed sense of purpose. I must prove to her that she is special to me, and that I can change. Maybe this thing could work between us. Bombarding thoughts juxtapose in my head, I still need time to process.

Looking around the garden I can't see anyone else appearing for the moment. I will make it look like I have just come back from my run, am sweaty and in need of a shower. That will put people off approaching me. Walking back round the edge of the maze I continue towards the house. Perhaps a few stretches by the pool will add to my ruse.

By chance I see Beatrice coming out of the French doors. God she's stunning, even in the morning after a late night. I could never get bored of enjoying the sight of her. She looks glowing, maybe the girls really are right and she does like me and the thought makes her happy too.

She spies me and changes course in my direction.

'Breakfast is ready in twenty minutes' she calls

I wait till we are closer to respond. When we come face to face I say

'Morning beautiful, you look gorgeous this morning, thank you for coming to find me' I plant a kiss on her lips and give her one of my big smiles.

She looks affronted. Oh. Well it must be my post jog sweaty body – yup definitely need a shower before breakfast.

'Well I didn't actually come to find you, specifically.' She says the last word deliberately pronouncing each syllable 'Holly asked me to come and tell you about breakfast. Claud said you weren't in your bedroom and she thought she saw you out here.'

Ah her pretend front. Now I know differently.

'It was really good of you to take the trouble to come outside. I've been for a run and need a shower though first. Care to join me?' I raise my eyebrows and flutter my lashes.

'Er no thanks I'll leave you to it and see you at breakfast'

She spins round and doesn't wait for me, hurrying to get back to the house, as if she is running away from me. She must be panicking, the temptation of shower sex is too much for her, which is why she ran off so quickly. She is still denying her feelings for me. Well now I know I must do something about that, find a way to tell her how I feel without her running a mile.

CHAPTER 20

Beatrice

God what is wrong with everyone this morning? Firstly Ursula and Holly were up before me, which is suspicious in itself. They are definitely up to something as they are behaving oddly.

Then Benedict was just being totally weird like he is still drunk from last night. Just a few hours ago he was being all macho and dominant (I clench at the thought, sweet Jesus...), and now he is behaving like a fool. Maybe running makes him lightheaded or something?

I just don't have a clue about what all this is about, but I intend to find out...

I had been woken up earlier by the sound of the house coming to life after its late night. I rolled onto my back, rubbed my eyes and winced as the welts on my bottom stung and reminded me of the marathon screw fest. That was by the longest mile, the hottest sex I have ever had in my life. Who knew I had a thing for a dominant male and bindings? Wow, not sure how I go back to normal life after that.

I stumbled into the shower and let the warm water soak over me. Rubbing the shower gel into my body and moaning in appreciation as I massaged it into my breasts and round my nipples, stroking and squeezing, carried away by the images and sensations flooding back from last night. My hands worked their way down and my fanny throbbed once at the anticipation of more attention.

No Beatrice not now I had told myself

I must snap out of this, this is not how I normally behave, I tried to divert my attention thinking of today and finished my shower in a more practical fashion. I scrubbed my teeth, brushed my hair and applied my makeup, with extra concealer under my eyes to cover up the dark patches resulting from too much wine and too little sleep. I regarded my reflection

You'll do

Hmmm extra make up attention, why did I do that? Normally I would be shuffling down in sweat pants and a messy pineapple hair up do.

Ok let's not over think this.

I needed to get through today and try out plutonic Benedict interaction so I can go back to work on Monday able to fully concentrate on the next case. With the confidence that I too can have mind-blowing sex of a weekend and be back working and giving my all during the following week.

I'd selected an off the shoulder summer floaty dress, it matched my mood or my trying to convey a carefree 'I can do this' image to myself. Shoving my feet into flip flops, I'd taken a deep breath and opened my bedroom door ready to face the world.

Holly and Ursula were busying themselves in the kitchen, laying out rashers of bacon on a grill and trimming sausages to cook for the troops for breakfast. When I had walked in they'd both looked like rabbits in head lights. In retrospect testament to the fact they were both up to something.

'Hi Bea' 'Morning!' they'd both trilled.

And gone back to being very busy.

Okaaaay

Needing a coffee I'd helped myself to the Nespresso machine. It had been empty of both water and spare capsules so filling it back up and finding more coffee had taken a few minutes.

There had been silence from the girls.

'Everyone good this morning? Enjoy last night? I'd asked them, leaning against the kitchen unit with arms crossed, as coffee buzzed into my cup.

'Yes great' they'd said in unison
'loved it thanks' said Holly

More silence. I'd taken my first sip of coffee, its reassuring warmth and caffeine kick giving me the boost to start my day.

'Ooh I can see Benedict outside' Holly announced breaking the quiet 'Claud had been looking for him and he wasn't in his bedroom. Looks like he's been running. Bea can you just pop out and let him know breakfast will be in twenty minutes?'

Hmmm not quite the confrontation I was hoping for first thing, but hey may as well start as I mean to go on.

'Sure'

I could do this .....

CHAPTER 21

Beatrice

The dining room had been cleared and the large central table restored to its position. It is covered in a white cloth and laid up for breakfast. Bowls of yoghurt, fruit salad, granola, jams, milk and orange juice, sit waiting for the guests to help themselves to easily. On the side table are a pile of plates and couple of heat trays, keeping warm all the components of a full English Breakfast, along with a toaster and a dish of plain and chocolate croissants. Perfect hang over breakfast.

The others file in one every few minutes, help themselves to the side table offerings and then sit down in the next spare seat. There is a subdued atmosphere, withdrawal headaches keeping the noise level low, ancestral portraits look down on everyone solemnly from the walls as ibuprofen is passed round to great relief.

I eat my breakfast in relative silence trying to avoid looking at Benedict who has come downstairs after his shower. He is looking rather delicious, I'd admired his backside sculpted by his jeans when he was helping himself to bacon and his fitted t shirt is showing off his ripped physique too perfectly. But he keeps trying to catch my eye, which is disconcerting and I can't play this game again.

'Good speech last night Leo' my father tries to make conversation.

'Yes really interesting.' Ursula endorses. 'I hadn't quite realised the scope of work the charity is involved in'

'Yes, thank you, I am really enjoying my involvement, as one of the ambassadors, and learning so much'

'Any one for tea?' Inno is circling the table with a pot offering top ups.

Claud, next to me, asks 'I presume you know the maze back to front as you have spent so much time here over the years?'

I reply 'actually I haven't tried it for years, one of those things you never get round to doing once you have done it as a child.'

Loosing myself in the maze could be the excuse I have been looking for to disappear for a while.

'Great I think we should all have a go after breakfast, good way to walk off our hangovers.'

Not quite what I had in mind.

Claud claps his hands and announces to the table. 'Prize for the first one to find the centre of the maze after breakfast'

There is a chorus of groans and someone shouts 'No thanks!'

Inno interjects 'Or as nothing is officially planned for today you can relax and enjoy the sun by the swimming pool.'

Everyone cheers and claps. Conversations start to buzz around the table.

I stand up to help clear, stack plates into the dishwasher and busy myself washing up. Inno is chatting away with me about some local gossip involving the pub landlord and a widow, she is such good fun, and I always enjoy spending time with her.

Presently Megan comes into the kitchen laughing. Inno looks at her a little unimpressed which she ignores.

'Oh my god it's so funny I think Claud and Peter are lost in the maze, or at least pretending to be. They are making such a performance of finding their way to the middle or out again. Mostly they are being ignored. You've got to come and witness this it's hilarious.'

Inno says to me 'you go on, don't miss out Bea, I'm happy to finish up in here.'

'Are you sure?' I check

'Yes definitely. Go on go!'

I follow Megan outside. It appears the supposed entertaining moment has passed as some of the others have started to settle themselves on the steamer chairs by the pool, chatting or looking at their phones.

'Oh sorry looks like we're too late' says Megan 'they may need help still. Why don't you go and find them. I've got to go and see to the horses. I'll see you later'

She leaves me and as I watch her go I see her head towards Boris, who has just come out from the house. They kiss in greeting and stand chatting to each other, unable to conceal their delight in each other and confirming my hunch they had got on rather well last night.

It all feels a bit odd, the others by the pool don't seem to be the slightest bit interested in helping Claud and Peter. Even Holly, who is sitting by the pool next to Ursula, doesn't seem too bothered that the new love in her life is lost in a maze. I deliberate whether to join them and see if there is any more gossip to catch up on but decide against it. They were behaving as if they are up to something and I don't want to feel like I am the only one not in the know. With nothing better to do but avoid Benedict, who is sat on his own by the pool, I decide to enter the maze. I am about the perfect height to enjoy the challenge of it as at five foot seven I am a couple of inches lower than the top of the hedge line. I really can't see over and am not able, at all, to cheat my way around. Confident I remember the right path I take the first left turn follow the path as it twists round, take a couple more left bends and arrive at a stone bench indicating a dead end. Never mind, the perfect opportunity, I can sit on the bench for a while and check-up what my friends are up to on social media. I scroll up on my phone and immerse myself in other people's lives.

Presently I hear male voices, it must be Claud and Pete coming back out, but my ears prick up as I tune into their conversation when I hear one name which stands out and catches my attention.

'Benedict'

Desperate to catch the thread of their conversation I put my phone on the bench and lean closer to the hedge

'.... most definitely he has feelings for Beatrice.' Sounds like Claud

What?!

I feel my heart beat take off.

'But how do you know? Normally he is flippant when it comes to women, moving on to the next one when he is done with the first' Pete is questioning

'I know him, remember I was there to pick up the pieces after Charlottegate. It's the reason he is like he is. She made him lose all trust in women and relationships'

Huh? This is news to me, my interest is really piqued now. I strain my head closer and shuffle along the hedge a little to keep up.

'Remind me what happened'

'He was a lot younger, still at Sandhurst and he fell in love. Don't you remember he used to facetime Charlotte every day when we were stationed in Germany?'

'Now you come to mention it I think I do'

'Then when we were first on leave he found out she had been shagging someone behind his back and his world fell apart.'

I clutch my hands to my chest, I had no idea.

'He went on the rampage in London after that fucking a different girl every night, got a taste for it and the rest is history. Well up until this weekend anyway.'

'And you reckon he is a changed man?'

'Undoubtedly, he is like a dog with a bone, I haven't seen him like this for years'

Oh my God, he has feelings for me? *Real feelings not just lustful ones?* I don't know how I feel about this, maybe it does explain his behaviour this morning.

'Do you think one of the girls should mention it to Beatrice? Surely she deserves to know.' Pete suggests.

'I don't think that would be a good idea, I am not sure how she would take it, she is so career obsessed and it might backfire on us and she'd use the knowledge to taunt him.'

'Yes maybe you are right, she's a fabulous girl but quite a lot to take on, it would take a brave man.'

They laugh.

This last comment makes me go cold, I didn't know people thought of me like that.

'What about Benedict – have you talked to him?'

'Good God no' Claud exclaims 'he's not the talking kind and

anyway he might not be impressed finding out we have been discussing him behind his back'

'It's a shame' says Pete 'Deep down he's a real gent and top bloke, very popular with a promising career ahead of him. They could be really happy'

'Yup well we've got to leave it alone, none of our business'

I hear one of them slap the other one on the back and they move off out of the maze. One of them bursts into laughter *Ugh?* I try to process what I have just heard.

I reel back to the bench and slump down my head in my hands. I feel numb all over, I am really shocked at what I have overheard. I had no idea that Benedict's previous behaviour was the result of having his heart broken, the thought is so distressing. He must have really suffered, poor him!

All that bravado and charm he exudes is just a mask to the broken man inside. Now he has feelings for me? I thought I was just sport to him and I would be the one to suffer after this weekend. That's why I put on a brave face and didn't want to appear to let him get to me. I had to pull the career card as a ruse to cover my own uncertainties. It saddens me that I am referred to as career obsessed and a lot to 'take on''. Am I really that bad? I mean I know I can be a bit outspoken and stubborn but aren't a lot of girls?

Could I be happy with him? Can I really have it both? The thought makes me feel hopeful and excited. He's good fun and bloody gorgeous too, which doesn't hurt and would be delicious to wake up to every morning. Maybe that's why he wanted to spend the night with me. I think he was going to suggest we meet up when we are back in London but he got interrupted by Boris last night.

With renewed hope I gather my phone and decide to abort the maze activity. I stand up and make my way back round away

from the stone bench. Two or three strides forward and I stop dead in my tracks, taken by surprise.
Benedict has found me, he stands stock still in front of me and as my eyes look into his sparkly blue ones, I see a question in them. My tummy twists.

CHAPTER 22

Benedict

Sitting by the pool was a bit boring. Well today it was because everyone else was paired up or in groups and much ensconced in their own business. Even Claud and Peter were behaving like new best friends, as if they have something going on that I am not party to. I saw them laughing and patting each other on the back, something must have been very entertaining for them. Well good for them I am so happy they have finally found each other. Bizarre that only last night Claud wanted to punch Pete in the face thinking he was cracking on to Holly and I ended up being the unfortunate one on the receiving end of his fury. Now they look like they want to do each other's make up or nails or something.

I have been absorbed in my own thoughts about Beatrice. Perhaps I just need to tell her how I feel. A risky tactic as she may run for the hills, but my feelings have been eating away at me and I have reached the point where I can't ignore them anymore. I conclude that I have to take the bull by the horns and brace myself for whatever outcome it may result in. She may stick to her guns and tell me where to go, her career being paramount on her priority list. Or maybe I can bring her round to at least meeting up after the weekend, take things slowly and see whether this could lead to something more. As I think it through I realise that I like her more than I initially wanted to admit to myself and the notion of her not wanting to see me anymore is painful beyond imagining.

She is in the maze and has been for a while. I think she is on her own, everyone else being either in the house still or by the pool. It is a good opportunity to have some privacy and for me to spill all. I make my way over, looking around at the hedges to work out my best way forward and checking behind me before I enter, thankfully it appears nobody is interested in where I am going. Now I just have the challenge of finding her, knowing I could come to a dead end and she could escape with my chance to talk delayed yet further. When I walk in through the opening my eye line, slightly above the top of the hedge, gives me a small advantage in my navigation.

Putting one foot in front of the other with no real clue which way to go I tentatively take the first left turn. As if my body is instinctively programmed to find her, we come face to face after two or three turns. I have made her jump and she stops dead in her tracks with an alarmed look on her face.

'Oh' she says 'You took me by surprise'

We stare at each other, I have suddenly become mute as if I might find an answer in her eyes and the silence drags between us. Eventually I come to my senses.

'I need to talk to you'
'Can I have a word?'

We say simultaneously, then both laugh, a little awkward.

'You first' she says

I take a deep breath, here goes 'I have been wanting to have a talk with you in private.'

'Oh' she says 'go on'

'I know that my behaviour hasn't exactly been exemplary at times over these last few days, certainly at the beginning of our stay here.'

'Hmm you don't say' she raises an eyebrow but more playfully than cross which gives me some courage to go on.

'For that I am truly sorry'

'Okaaay' she draws out 'apology accepted. I didn't exactly try to stop you too forcibly either, so I can take some of the blame.'

Images of her in submissive positions come to mind and I am momentary thrown off course. Why does my dick interrupt me at such a crucial time as this? *Concentrate Benedict*

'I don't think either of us originally had any intention to' I try to think of an appropriate word 'interact in the way we have, given that you didn't like me and my record for anything more than short term liaisons has been sketchy at best. I appreciate I was playing to type on that last point too.'

She looks like she is about to say something, so I plough on.

'The thing is I couldn't get you out of my head, I kept wanting more. I couldn't ignore the chemistry we have, but not only that I enjoy your company ...... a lot in fact. I love spending time with you and don't want to stop.'

She takes a step closer to me.

'The thought of not being able to enjoy your company, after this weekend, is painful to me, agony in fact. You see you have gotten through to me and I don't want to let you go..... I don't think my heart would take it' I add admitting out loud to myself for the first time.

She is so close and looks up to me. Unshed tears glisten in her eyes but she is smiling through them.

'Do you think you could bring yourself to see me again, when we are back in London, next week even' she doesn't move 'please say yes.'

Then she reaches up and puts her arms up around my neck

'Yes'

Relief floods through me as her lips move up to mine and she stands on tiptoes, barely able to reach she gives me a soft kiss.

'Oh thank God!' I say as I fling my arms around her and lift her off the ground in a sort of kiss/embrace hug. She laughs joyfully. 'Thank you thank you thank you!'

I put her back down but don't want to let her go so my arms stay around her and we smile goofily at each other.

'What about you, did you want to say something?' She had said she wanted a word too. For a second I experience doubt that she might change her mind.

'Well it was kind of along the same track actually.' She considers what she will say 'I think I have been putting up a bit of an icy front because I didn't want to get hurt. Then I thought I could try to channel my inner you and have a bit of fun this weekend, because it has been fun, and move on next week without any regret. I believed if I could do the sex but not do the affection bit I would prevent myself from getting attached.'

She blushes a little, which is totally adorable.

'Then I overheard something this morning that made me realise I had lost that battle and had developed feelings.'

Listening to her open up to me gives me a buzz of warmth. Hang on a minute ...

'Did you say you overheard something?' I start to think this feels a little coincidental

Her guilty expression looks like she has been caught with her hand in the sweetie jar. 'I absolutely didn't mean to but couldn't help it, the conversation was going on so close'

'Hmmm'

'Oh God sorry I had never intended to eavesdrop.'

'No don't worry it's not you, you see I also overheard a conversation earlier too' remembering the laughing I had heard afterwards, which didn't register at the time as suspicious but does now. 'We may have been the subjects of a ruse.'

'Are you sure?'

'Well who did you overhear?'

'Pete and Claud, why?'

'I overheard Holly and Ursula talking, it was earlier when I was coming back from my run, your name stood out when it was mentioned and I couldn't tear myself away from the other side of the hedge. Now I remember they were giggling afterwards and I think they wholly intended their conversation for the benefit of my ears.'

'The buggers!' she exclaims 'I knew they were up to something, everyone was acting so strangely this morning.' She looks back up to me.

'Do you mind?' I ask

She considers for a second 'No, no not now, maybe we needed a push to make us realise our true feelings.'

'I think you are right' I look at her tenderly noticing for the first time a few freckles dotted over her nose and her eyes more turquoise than blue with little gold flecks in them. They are looking deep into mine and it makes my heart lurch 'you are so amazing' I plant a kiss on her lips, that familiar charge comes alive between us and I don't pull away. Our mouths open letting each other explore further, soft and inviting our tongues move and collide, I relish the sensation, more intimate than before, it feels like a prelude to what the rest of our bodies want to follow with.

I scoop her into my arms feeling a bit like a romantic hero. Backing up to the stone bench and gently lowering myself to a sitting position she sits across my lap. Our lips don't break contact as we continue our slow languid kiss. Arousal swells within me and my erection strains against my fly, the bulge pressing against the base of her back. She reaches behind her and puts a hand over my crotch, I groan, appreciating the small comfort her touch gives me.

'Someone is looking for more attention.' She giggles

'It's what you do to me.' I put her hair over one shoulder and kiss along her neckline. She moves closer to give me better access, her body vibrating from her little pleasure moans, it makes my erection even harder. Standing up and removing her panties, she bends forward and undoes the button and fly on my jeans. I enjoy her taking control, I am commando underneath and thanking my lack of underwear for the access it affords her now. My dick's delight at its new release is amplified as Beatrice gets down on her knees, rests her forearms on my thighs and positions her head close to my cock. She licks her lips slowly and her tongue extends out and circles its peak, then she dives closer still, her head on one side, and draws a path with her tongue up and down its length. I exhale heavily, the feeling a teasing overture, she is so hot when she gets dirty. Glancing up at me, her eyes smoky with arousal and her red hair cascading onto my thighs, my tempting she-devil, her expression looks like she is enjoying the power she has over me at this moment. Her mouth shaped in the perfect O takes in my shaft fully and she drags her lips down its length.

'Jesus Christ that feels so good'

I feel it hit the back of her throat. *Oh Happy Days.*

'Oh fuck!'

Then it is pulled back through her lips, the firm silky friction giving me such intense pleasure. With slow precision she moves her head up and down and I watch in awe the vision of her plump lips circling my dick as it appears and disappears inside her. If I think that it couldn't be a more perfect moment in my life she adds her tongue to the mix. Tensing the tip of her small muscle I can feel its path along my penis as it is drawn up and down. I want to grab her head and drive myself in and out of her mouth in a frenzy, my frustration at wanting a release I need to be inside her, the feeling heightened as she feels and strokes around my balls gently massaging and inducing that familiar drawing up, bracing for an impending orgasm.

'I want to fuck you' I demand and she withdraws her mouth and looks up to me licking off a drop of precum from the corner of her lip, I am totally done for 'Sit on me now'

'Condom?'

'Back pocket'

She reaches behind me fumbling in my jeans and bringing the foil packet round offers it to my mouth. I grasp it in my teeth and ripping the packet open draw it over my erection.

'Now sit on me'

She opens her legs and hovers over me circling her clit over my head, I can see she is already aroused, her trimmed pubic hair moist with her own juices. Impatiently I rock my hips for a few turns teasing her closer before she impales herself around me.

We both sigh, the feeling pure bliss and she stills holding the position, totally connected and utterly lost. Beatrice is in control as she dictates the slow deliberate pace and moves her hips up and down. I put my hands around her waist, I am iron hard and want to savour this heavenly oblivion she takes me to. Her pace increases and she puts both hands on my jaw looking directly into my eyes to spur me on. I drive into her hard, holding her firmly down onto me with each thrust of my hips. At the final force I climax with a shudder and my whole body shakes. My teeth clench as her body milks mine and she throws her head back and orgasms, stifling a scream.

'Wow' she says as she looks back up and into my eyes. I put my arms tighter around her instinctively drawing her as close to me as our skewered position allows, feeling a sentiment which takes me by surprise.

She is mine and I want to protect her

For the first time in a very long time I feel a contentment I didn't think I would ever truly believe I would have. She is fucking perfect, which is both mind blowingly wonderful and totally terrifying at the same time.

CHAPTER 23

Benedict

I am humming with a post orgasmic high as we straighten ourselves out and pull our underwear back on, I cannot wipe the jubilant 'I've just been given a blow job' smile off my face. To maintain our contact we hold hands as we walk back round to the exit of the maze. Before taking the final step and launching ourselves into the scrutiny of our friends I have a thought.

'Hang on' I turn Beatrice towards me, pull her in for a hug and try to wipe off the giveaway grin. Inhaling the unique smell of her hair I want to hold onto the moment for a bit longer and enjoy our special bubble of newly admitted feelings for each other.

'Hmmm this is lovely' she says nuzzling into my chest 'I could stay like this all day.

'Me too' I agree 'Listen I have been thinking. I think we should wait before we let on to everyone that we have discovered their little plot.' She looks back up at me 'Firstly I want to savour us, it's our business and I am not ready to share our newly acknowledged 'us' with the rest of the household, not just yet.'

'I know what you mean, I feel the same.'

'Secondly we may find the opportunity to get our own back on their scheming, I am not sure how yet but let's just keep this on the 'back burner' until an opportunity arises.'

'Ok sounds good.' She leans back into my arms for a last hug. 'We should go back separately' I say 'you go on ahead of me.' She stands up on tiptoes and gives me a peck on the lips, God she's delicious.

I tear myself away feeling like a stubborn band aid, missing the loss of her presence next to me and her touch as soon as I step back into the broad sunlight.

Claud, Pete and Leo are together by the pool, I decide to join them and find out what bollocks they are all talking about, a necessary distraction to stem the loss of not having my hot flame haired obsession at my side.

'I'm going to head off in good time in the morning, I need to get a few things sorted tomorrow back at home' Pete is saying as I join them

Claud responds 'I'm trying to persuade Holly to come back to London with me, but she needs to check with Beatrice first who was originally going to drive her back.' He looks up 'Oh hi Ben don't worry there's plenty of room for all three of us'

'Great I love being a gooseberry, thought I could feel those little green hairs sprouting from my chin.' I rub my chin for extra effect. I don't mind in the least and besides it gives me the perfect excuse to go back with Beatrice but its good sport witnessing Claud feel guilty. It's about time that he is the one, not me, changing plans because of a girl.

Pete offers 'I could give you a lift if you don't mind squashing in the back of the car, it will give Claud the chance of some privacy with Holly.' The thought of spending any time, let alone a couple of hours, in the company of John is abysmal. 'I am sure you don't mind getting back to London sooner than planned, gives you a chance to organise your next one night stand!'

They all think this is hilarious.

'A man can change' I jump, rather hastily to my defence, 'anyway I might not be in the mood.'

Claud looks at me, he has clocked my too swift retort.

'Of course, are you ok Mountant you look out of sorts?' Leo asks looking concerned

'I think he's in love!' Claud taunts giving me a nudge.

'Impossible!' Pete exclaims 'Love and Mountant never go together in the same sentence.'

'Very funny' *Great now I am the subject of their sport*

Leo is studying my face too 'Your cheek is red, do you have toothache or something?' he points to the left side of my face.

My hand flies to cover it and rubbing the spot, I wonder if it is Beatrice's lipstick or maybe I'm just being paranoid it's actually where Claud lumped me last night.

Claud is laughing at Leo's sincerity and my discomfort 'I'm telling you, he's definitely in love!'

Pete joins in, his irony is blatant 'Do you know there is definitely something about you Mountant today, you are looking different, is it because you haven't shaved?' He is looking at both sides of my face 'or maybe because you have!'

'Oh yes' says Leo 'it makes you look younger, I think'

Claud won't drop his teasing 'Shaving and making an effort further evidence he has fallen in love'

'And a stressful look on his face, a tell-tale sign, it's a given.' Pete agrees

'Exactly! And I know who with!' Claud is really in his stride now so I give up, crossing my arms with a resigned expression and let him have his moment.

'Do you think she is unsuspecting?' Pete adds

Laughing and throwing his arm around my shoulder Claud says 'either that or she knows and has absolutely no idea what he is capable of!'

Believe me she does

I've had enough of the newbies and want to take the opportunity to talk to the Colonel about mentoring my next step up the ladder. Might not be the best timing but I may not get another convenient moment. 'Leo can I have a word? I wonder if I could pick your brains.' I ask him 'I was going to head back to the house, would you mind?' *And leave these hobby horses to it.*

We return to the house together and just before I head out of earshot I hear more jeering from Claud and Pete and one of them says the name 'Beatrice' loudly and they burst into laughter ... the sods.

CHAPTER 24

Beatrice

After my revelation in the maze I head back to the house to find Holly. We spend a relaxing afternoon together, either in each other's bedrooms preparing for our return tomorrow or out by the pool. Swimming and enjoying the last rays of afternoon sun before heading back to another week of office lighting and London smog. I don't mention Benedict and she doesn't ask about him. I want to enjoy my secret to myself for a bit longer, the revelation is new to me and the fact that I have really fallen for him, being the one thing I reverently vowed I wouldn't do, I am not sure how I truly feel about everything.

That I have feelings for Benedict, I am in no doubt, but how this will work in my life day to day I am still at a loss to imagine. I am excited to spend time with him in the future, these last few days have felt like a parallel reality and any thought of not seeing him leaves me feeling fretful. Thinking about him gives me a warm fuzzy feeling and I want to selfishly relish this on my own, just for now.

Holly is dreamy about Claud and also excited for what their future will hold. Whilst hanging out in her bedroom, I'd lain across a bedroom chair with my head on one armrest and my legs draped over the other, she was lying on her bed with her feet up against the wall. We flicked through gossip magazines and aired our thoughts, our non-confrontational positions al-

lowed us to speak freely without having the reactions of facial expression and eye contact. I was happy to hear about her thoughts, feelings and plans, she seems to have made her mind up, very resolutely since last night, that he is serious boyfriend material.
She did try to question me on my situation, which I brushed off with an 'Oh you know me' non-committal answer. I know that she knows something is going on but she is letting me have my space knowing I will talk when I am ready.

I haven't seen much of Benedict this afternoon, he was with Leo for a while in his office and then I think all the boys were playing snooker in the billiards room after that. I believe he wants to protect our secret, until we are ready to face up to the reactions from our friends and family, giving himself time to get his head around the whole 'us' thing. Now I know a small snippet of what he went through with Charlotte I understand his need to process, the undealt with buried pain from their relationship must be forefront in his mind. He will need to move on accepting that Charlotte's betrayal is a hurtful memory which he can leave firmly in the past, then he will be truly ready to embark on a relationship with me.

The plan for later is a 'last supper' all together before we head back at various times tomorrow. Inno and Holly are on cooking duty and I have offered to peel potatoes and be general dog's body. It is therapeutic sitting at the island in the kitchen, perched on a high stool, with a large chopping board in front of me, mindlessly peeling carrots, chopping beans and switching off to enjoying the chat from Inno. She is good company, not at all intimidating and very easy going. She never judges, just accepts and councils if need be or laughs infectiously, always seeing the humour and turning a bleak situation into something much easier to deal with. I think her experience as a nurse, from her former life, has given her the tools to make people feel at ease and she treats everyone with dignity and respect. She must have witnessed some horrors during her career at the hospital so I understand how she can see the bright side to our petty woes, even so she is never belittling of them.

I am absorbed in my vegetable prep and friendly chat between the three of us when out of the corner of my eye two faces I don't recognise peer in through the kitchen window. They look a little intimidating and it takes me by surprise, I drop the small knife I am using along with some of the beans which scatter in every direction on the floor.

'Bother' I react 'Sorry' I bend down to pick up the escapees as Inno and Holly both look towards what has alarmed me.

'Ahh Dave and Vince!' Inno comes dashing round the island wiping her hands on her apron and gestures at the window.

'Come in, come in!' she exclaims pointing and moving towards the back door from the utility room.

Holly and I look at each other, she appears puzzled as to who our new guests could be, Inno explains in a loud whisper just before she leaves the kitchen.

'Dave and Vince are from the village, they head up the neighbourhood watch gang. It's a new volunteer group formed mostly of retired residents who keep a look out for us all since there has been a spate of garage burglaries.'

'Welcome, welcome!' She is saying as they enter the kitchen. 'Come through .... No leave your shoes on ...... yes honestly'. 'Cup of tea? Holly would you put the kettle on?'

'That would be lovely' says the shorter man

'This is Dave, Dave my daughter Holly who I am sure you have met before and my niece Beatrice.' She introduces us all 'And Vince, how are you?'

They are both dressed in baggy tweed jackets. Vince is about double the height of Dave and looks slightly awkward, stooping with his height in an attempt to be on a level with the rest of us. He blushes a little when Inno turns her focus on him, poor man is uncomfortable with the attention, and says quickly in his regional accent.

'Very well thank you Mrs Upparrr' bobbing his head.

Inno leans on the aga rail waiting for the kettle to boil. 'Vince is somewhat of a local hero' she tells us 'he chased off a potential thief who had already broken the padlock off the Ayrton's shed. It was about three weeks ago now wasn't it?'

I think she is trying to readdress the balance between them as Dave seems to be the one in charge and appears to want to take the lead, he is shuffling on the spot and wanting a bit of the limelight so he replies. 'Yes three weeks and two days, it was a Thursday evening that Vince appended the potentchul fief.' His choice of words are a little confused compounded by his country accent.

I catch Holly's eye and see her mouth twitch as she had also spotted the incorrect wording.'

The kettle boils, Inno turns round fills the tea pot and sets out some mugs. 'Was he threatening or aggressive to you Vince?' She goes to the fridge to retrieve the jug of milk.

Dave replies again on Vince's behalf 'Luckily when Vince shone his torch on him the velon scarpered.' Vince doesn't say much just joins in with lots of head bobbing and agreeing yesses and grunts.

I see Holly's body start to shake as she turns round and pretends to look for something in the cupboard. Inno ignores her, swirling the teapot and pouring tea into the mugs.

'Sugar, Milk?'

Dave says 'Milk and two sugars please, Vince'l have the same thank you.'

Inno hands the mugs to the men 'And has there been any trouble since?'

Dave and Vince both take slurpy sips of their hot tea. Dave answers 'Not since then but we have been extra breedy-eyed at night time, after the pubs close and stuff. We can't rest on our laulels just yet'

Holly's infectious giggle stifling has gotten to me, my eyes start to water and I am about to put my teeth through my lips I am biting them so hard trying to not burst into laughter. How Inno remains so unaffected I cannot fathom.

'Girls' she says like an old school mistress 'I forgot to ask Dad to bring out the fire pit for later can you find him, we need logs as well, you'll both need to help him.

Tell me Dave .....' she turns to the men.

Holly dashes out of the room, I manage to just about hold it together and smile at Dave and Vince to acknowledge my departure and then follow her. Once we are through in the kitchen door and hopefully out of earshot we burst out laughing, bending double and holding our stomachs.

'Oh my god, I couldn't help it, I am in so much trouble, and mum is going to kill me!'

'It's your fault!' I say my tears streaming 'you got me going too'

We straighten and take deep breaths trying to compose ourselves. I'm trying to think of serious things, anything but poor Dave's misuse of the language.

Holly stands up and away from the wall inhaling and exhaling heavily 'Think we'd better try to find Dad.'

Outside we track down Leo who is directing operations. We are going to eat Al fresco this evening so the boys are moving tables from around the pool to make one long one together under the arbour. Ursula is collecting chairs from various places to set at the table. I subtly seek out Benedict and as if my body is tuned to his presence, I clock him moving around without allowing myself to overtly goggle him.

'Dad we've got to get the fire pit out.' Holly declares loudly 'Bea and I can do it, can you just remind me where it is?'

'In the back of the pool heater shed.' Leo answers loudly in reply from the other side of the pool.

'We need logs too.'

'I can help' Benedict, having overheard, offers and walks towards us. Just his closeness makes my body come alive, if I catch his eye I will give myself away. My eye-level is at his pecks which is a magnificent enough sight. I can see them defined and rock hard behind the loose drape of his cotton jersey t shirt and I want to reach out and run my fingers over them.

'Great thanks' says Holly 'Come with us, there is a stack on the side of the shed'

'Sure' he follows us over, catching up behind me, I can feel him get closer but can't do anything about it. As we get to the shed I feel the ghost of a stroke on my hip and he says 'Hi' barely audible in my ear. My skin tingles both from his touch and the warm sensation on the back of my neck. I smile over my shoulder.

'It would be great if you could heap up a few next to the fire pit so we have a supply for the evening.' Holly says oblivious, pointing to the log pile.

Benedict starts picking off logs and holding them in the crook of his arm, his toned biceps strain at their work, the t shirt's short sleeve finishing high enough to show them off to their best. Holly notices too and for a moment the pair of us gawp in admiration. He is so onto us, looking up with a smug grin and saying. 'Everything alright?'

Holly mortified at being caught ogling, blushes and turns away to enter the shed stammering 'Yes .... perfect .... thank you .... lets see if we can find the fire pit Bea.'

We walk into the shed and the hum of the pool filter system covers her voice as she says under her breath 'Damn we were so busted, and the conceited sod knows it!' I giggle. Two days ago I would never have reacted like this, Holly looks at me, but then giggles too her face reddening and her eyes watering, we both have to take more deep breaths to stop ourselves having another hysteria laughing fit.

I can smell a warm wood shed smell as we duck cobwebs and avoid plant pots to get to the back and find the fire pit along with a box of outdoor fairy lights and some candle lanterns. We pile the whole lot into the pit and carry the now heavier load back out. I enjoy the productive team effort, amongst us all, to prepare for later. Holly and I weave lights in and out of the arbour trellis, hang some of the lanterns and put others around and on the table. Ursula has found seat cushions and is placing these on the chairs.

Meanwhile Inno has come out with a rickety trolley laden with glasses, cutlery and some bottles of beer. She instructs Boris and Conrad to lay the table, showing them first how she would like it done. Then she busies herself opening the bottles of beer and handing them out to those who have finished their tasks. We sit down two or three to a sun lounger, stretch our legs out and enjoy the balmy evening, basking in the last of the warm sun rays as it dips lower in the sky.

Ursula, having finished her beer, is the first to stand up 'I'm going for a shower before supper'

'Me too' says Holly, others take her lead and we all troop back to our rooms to get ready.

Back in my room I relax in the bath, having added bath oil, indulging in the verbena scented warm water and not wanting to get out. Savouring every last moment of my stay with that feeling that it will come to an end all too soon tomorrow.

I decide to wear my blue dress tonight, I bought it not long before the weekend and haven't worn it before. It is short-ish, the hem finishing just above my knees with a dropped waist and a wide v-neck. There are cut outs on the sleeves and it is loose fitting, it makes me feel relaxed and sexy not something I usually consider myself to be. I add to my look some large hooped gold ear rings, an armful of bangles and leave my hair in its slightly mad wavy state. I make up my eyes with smoky shadow and thicker kohl and finish off spritzing on some perfume.

There is a knock at my door, I assume it is Holly or Ursula so I shout 'Come in!' from the bathroom, not looking round as I apply some lip gloss in the mirror. I hear them enter and then a drawn out low whistle makes me turn. Benedict is standing in my room looking through the bathroom door apparently admiring what he sees.

'Wow you look seriously hot!'

He has scrubbed up pretty well too as the sight of him in an open necked fitted navy shirt, tight dark jeans and loafers has my tummy turning somersaults. His sleeves are rolled up to the elbows giving a delicious view of his strong forearms, I sashay over and stand in front of him. He holds me with both hands on my hips, looks into my eyes and bends down for a feather soft kiss. I all but swoon.

'Ummm that's so nice' is all I can muster in my response.

'I came in to see if you were ready to go down for dinner' his hands start to move up my body 'now I want to take you and those sexy come fuck me eyes to bed. I am torn as to which one to do, the bed option being by far preferable in this moment to me and my dick.'

And to me too 'We can't!' I reluctantly remove his hands from me 'I am supposed to be handing round canapes and helping and aren't you on drinks duty?'

'Ugh yes you are right, at least one of us is sensible' his shoulders slump for effect 'You look absolutely gorgeous by the way' he gives me a peck on the cheek 'Well then If you are ready shall we?' he offers his bent arm to which I thread my hand in, relishing the small chance to feel my fingers along the tautness of his bicep.

How did I get like this in just three days??? I have SO changed.

We leave my room and I am thankful no one is around. I absolutely love the feeling of being on his arm but still not quite ready to admit that to all here. By taking the back stairs at least we are not conspicuous by being together. As we reach the bottom I dive into the hustle and bustle of the kitchen and Benedict peels off in search of his job making pre dinner drinks for us all.

Inno spies me walk in 'Ahh Bea perfect timing!' she hands me a large plate of smoked salmon on little squares of brown bread 'Can you take these around? Hang on ...' She squirts on some lemon juice 'There you go'

'They look delicious' I try one 'hmm really good' with a mouthful I take the plate and head through the back to the swimming pool area.

Now the sun has gone down it looks magical outside. The fire pit is burning, the flames dancing skywards, their glow reflecting off the few faces standing around it. The fairy lights are glimmering in and out of the roses climbing the trellis and the lanterns have been lit making the glassware and cutlery shimmer in mirroring the moving light. Someone has put some music on, top 20 stuff which adds to the party atmosphere.

I offer my nibbles around to appreciative thanks and take a glass of prosecco which Benedict hands to me, his fingers stroking mine as he passes the glass. With my hands full I can't react to the fireworks erupting on my skin I just have to endure his cheeky wink as he moves and gives glasses to both Holly and Ursula.

We enjoy our pre dinner drinks then sit down to a delicious supper of beef wellington and sticky toffee pudding along with some delectable red wine that Leo has generously served from his extensive collection in the cellar. There is a relaxed ease with everyone this evening, the result of three days all together and shared experiences to relive and discuss.

Every once in a while I catch Benedict looking tenderly at me his gorgeous blue eyes twinkling before his gaze gets torn away to concentrate on what Inno, who he is sitting next to, is chatting about. I have Conrad on one side of me but his attention is focussed to John on his left and Leo on my right, who keeps getting up and down to fill up wine glasses so I find myself sometimes with no one to talk to. I don't mind this, it gives me a chance to look around and soak up the happy images of friends and family, feeling blessed and imprinting this special night on my memory.

Ironically this unforgettable supper party will turn out to be the event of the calm before the storm.

CHAPTER 25

Benedict

Now I have admitted to myself that I have feelings for Beatrice my heart is on full throttle and I crave to be with her all the time. I feel a possessiveness towards her bordering on obsessive as I now want to be the one and only one to make her laugh, fulfil her waking needs then fall asleep with her every night and fill every dream. I have spent this evening a little frustrated, only being able to admire her, in her sexy blue dress, from across the table and my mind and body are humming with the desire to have her all to themselves.

After supper the company disperses away from sitting round the table. Some pull their chairs to nearer the fire pit to carry on drinking and talking. Some move around the table and form a new conversation, John, Pete and Claud being one of these groups. Beatrice and Megan, despite Inno insisting otherwise, help take a few loads of dirty plates and glasses to the kitchen. To keep myself closer to Beatrice I help too. After a couple of trips I hang around outside the kitchen and grab Beatrice as she exits. Without saying a word I lead her through the house and we giggle like naughty children as we make our escape up the front stairs to avoid the main traffic of helpers who are going to and fro at the back of the house.

I pull her all the way to my bedroom and once inside with the door firmly closed I draw her into a tight embrace.

'Thank God at last I have you all to myself' I say with relief kissing the top of her head.

She looks up at me 'it did feel a long time at the table with no one to talk to, Conrad's attention was firmly focused to John and Uncle Leo was on wine duty. But it was a kind of special meal.' She pauses as if she is thinking about what she will say next 'This weekend has been so much more than I ever imagined it would be, I don't want it to end. It's as if I'm in a dream, I will wake up tomorrow and it will all have been a figment of my imagination.' Her gaze imploring mine for reassurance from her confession. I can't find the right words to express how I feel without terrifying her and admit too much too soon. It's been a long time since I was in a relationship and I am rusty at being able to say what I feel. Chat up lines and seduction having been my chosen subject for far too long.

Instead I reassure her in the way I know best. 'Come here you' I pull her close and hug her to my chest, her warmth and delicious scent already so familiar, makes my body feel contented, like coming home after a long time away. We fit together like the final pieces of a puzzle and she feels exactly perfect folded into my arms. It doesn't take long, with her body so close to mine, for that familiar creep of desire to lick its way up my body and I feel stirrings down below. So in tune to each other, I know Beatrice is reacting to our closeness as she shuffles her position a little and looks up at me.

I lower my head and our lips find each other and softly touch, she stands on tiptoes to get closer access, puts her arms around my neck, and her tongue joins mine and commences a slow leisurely dalliance. We pull slightly apart for a moment, I take her lower lip between my teeth and gently nibble and pull away. She moans in pleasure. Planting little kisses along her jaw, I massage her earlobe delicately with my front teeth and breathe in her unique smell my nose muzzling in the soft hair behind.

'That feels SO good' she coos

She turns me on so much I have to keep myself in check, I don't want to rush things. Tonight I want to make every second count, enjoy every inch of her.

'I want you so much' I say 'I don't want to just play and fuck, tonight I want more than that, I want us to make love.'

Wasting no time she unbuttons my shirt, emitting a low purring hum. Her fingers trace across my chest as she pulls the shirt apart over my shoulders and down my arms. Once I am free of the sleeves her hands come back and she feels over the contours of my pecks and abs, her fingers gliding down and up, across to my arms and around my biceps.

'I have been wanting to do this all evening.' She chuckles 'it hasn't disappointed, the feel being every bit as good as the sight of you in that t-shirt earlier'.

I love that she had needy thoughts about me. Her touch and words make me glow inside.

Continuing their journey her fingers stroke gently down my chest and stomach to the top of my jeans, tracing a path round above the belt which she undoes along with the button on my jeans.

She looks back up at me as if asking for permission to reach in. I give her the briefest of nods and my eyes urge her onwards.

Her hand works its way under the denim and finds my rock hard erection, her fingers feel around it but she is unable to gain a full grasp as my fitted jeans are hampering further foreplay. She attempts to push them over my hips so my hands cover hers and help the impetus to take them all the way down. I step out and look to see Beatrice staring at me her eyes wide.

'Holy fuck!' she exclaims, which I take as a compliment. I work out and train hard, which to this point has been totally worthwhile just to enjoy the admiration on her face.

My erection begs for more attention. I step closer and stoop down to kiss her further, our tongues join in and we continue our embrace as I reach down, grasp both sides of her dress and pull it up and over her head, Beatrice obliging by lifting her arms. Our mouths pull apart just long enough to get the dress off before slamming back together and continuing their assault. I reach behind her back and unclip her bra which she wriggles out of, not wishing to miss the view of her freed breasts I pull back and take in their glorious sight, then dive down to bury my face.

'So perfect' I say just before I suck one nipple into my mouth and circle the top with my tongue.

'Oh yes' Beatrice encourages as I take the other one drawing it into my mouth then pulling back slowly, my fingers teasing the first one to keep it pebbled. They both pucker and for a second I stare like a horny teenager, then go back for more mouth action as Beatrice throws her head back, gasping with pleasure.

I manoeuvre us both towards the bed and with one hand fling back the top cover. She takes her cue to lie down and I climb onto the bed and over her. I look down, she is the most delectable offering, her creamy white skin looks so smooth and my palm twitches with the temptation to leave a few rosy reminders. But I check myself again, determined this time to keep our loving vanilla, we can do both and it doesn't always need to be about my desire to dominate.

I pull down her panties, then run my nails all the way up the inside of her thighs to her pussy and play with her clit, which is already swollen and glistening.

'Bloody hell' I react as she grinds herself onto my fingers eager to get more traction.

'Hmmm' She moans 'that feels good' she is so wet. I grab a condom from the bedside table and as I roll it on she opens her legs wider to accommodate me.

I enter her slowly trying to be gentle, I am in awe of her, treating her like a china doll, withdrawing back without pushing all the way in, worried as I am so turned on I might be too much for her.

'It's ok, I won't break, you don't have to be too gentle!' she says needing more.

With permission given, my pace get stronger and I push in and out further and firmer. Her arms reach around me and her fingers dig into my shoulder blades, anchoring us together, we fuck closer like this for a few minutes, moving together our rhythm like a rolling sea, my assault gaining momentum with every thrust. Panting in time with our movements her arms come back around and I grab each wrist in turn and secure them down with one hand above her head so she is more stretched out. Her eyes close in concentration but I am damned if she is going to be enjoying this on her own.

'Look at me' I command thrusting in with more force, her eyes spring open 'I want to see your eyes when you come for me' and her big blues look deep into mine. 'You are so fucking beautiful' She is my warrior goddess, all mine to revere and make love to. 'I just can't get enough of you' my muscles burn and my adrenaline is pumping as my hips continue their invasion. Spurred on as Beatrice's pants turn into whimpers then small screams, I am balls deep and my cock can't go any further. I am so close.

'I'm going to come!' Beatrice yells

'Fuuuuck!' I shout as I orgasm with such an intensity my ejaculations go on and on emptying into her as pleasure in its entirety consumes my body.

I slump onto to her, our bodies slick with heat and sweat and our foreheads touch, neither of us wanting to pull away needing to feel our closeness as we stay tied together for as long as we can.

'You are so amazing' I kiss her. She smiles, puts her arms around me and gently massages with her finger tips across my shoulder blades, all the time gazing into each other eyes enjoying the sight of each other, wanting to prolong this blissful moment.

Beatrice stifles a small yawn, I have exhausted her, which is my cue to pull out.

'I'm sleepy now' she chuckles almost a little embarrassed

'Hang on' I deal with the condom and then turn back and pull her into me, her back against my chest. 'That's better'

She sighs contentedly 'I could do this every night...' We both still, I hear her inhale sharply. 'I mean that hypothetically' she adds quickly, assuming I would panic at the thought. Instead it feels like the best suggestion and the thought gives me a glow of happiness but I am not ready to voice exactly that, just yet.

'It's ok, I know what you mean ..... Let's sleep.'

'Are ok with me staying here?'

'Don't be silly. I wouldn't let you leave even if you wanted to.' I hug her a bit tighter to me.

'Hmmm' she replies and it is not long before I hear her slow steading breathing, she has fallen asleep.

I feel elated lying with her in my arms and am just about to drop off when I hear some rattling against the windows. I ignore the noise to start with, assuming it is just the wind or climbing plants scratching the glass. But my ears stay alert and prick up when I hear voices coming from outside and more rattling. *Is someone throwing stones at my window?*
Reluctantly I pull my arm out as gently as possible from under Beatrice, she rolls further on her side and snuggles down deeper into the mattress. I tiptoe to the window with my hand covering my privates and peer round the curtain. Pete is gesticulat-

ing with his arm for me to come down.

'Oh God, crap timing Pete, what now?' I mutter to myself.

I pull on some sweats that are draped over the chair and slip out of my room to find out what is going on.

Exiting the orangery I find Claud pacing in a fit of agitation with Pete trying to placate him and John standing by.

'What the fuck is going on?' I ask

John answers 'I made a discovery this evening, I couldn't believe what I had overheard but then I witnessed it with my own eyes. With my allegiance lying with my brother and his colleague I had to share what I was witnessing.'

'Ok cut the preamble .... go on' wanting him to get to the point.

'I discovered that Holly is being disloyal.'

'Disloyal?' I question in disbelief. *Is this another of his tricks?*

'I was enjoying a smoke out here, under those windows' he gestures towards the bedroom windows of the east wing which includes Beatrice's 'before turning myself in for the night, when I saw through that open window' he points again to what I assume he means is Holly's bedroom 'Boris and Holly making out, oblivious that they were being watched.'

'I don't believe it' I say 'you must have got it wrong are you sure it was Holly?'

'I went indoors to get Pete and Claud as I knew they were having a nightcap in the kitchen. I wanted them to see with their own eyes what I believed I was seeing.' He seems to be revelling in this charade. 'As we all looked up we could see the back of Holly's head and heard Boris quite clearly through the open window definitely say 'Holly' and Claud confirmed it was Holly's bedroom window.'

I am at a loss, this all seems really bizarre and just doesn't sound like something Holly would do, even the short time I have known her it seems totally out of character. Plus Boris had hooked up with Megan. I know he has a taste for threesomes, but he must have made fast work of chatting up Holly, and that in itself is the least plausible notion, he's not exactly charm personified.

Poor Claud looks totally distraught, I really feel for him. I would be devastated if I were in his shoes, given how quickly he fell for Holly. That old feeling of having been cheated on makes your whole body feel heavy with the weight of having been deceived and sends your mind to a dark place.

'I'm so sorry mate' I say to Claud 'There must be some explanation, don't do anything rash tonight let's see how things pan out in the morning. You must give Holly a chance to explain.' I try to give him a sympathetic hug which he shrugs off. He's drunk, which doesn't help him see reason and only fuels his anger.

'I won't do anything tonight but I fully intend to shame her in the morning ..... the slag!'

He pulls away from us, I know he's hurting as he stomps back into the house. His arm bashes into the frame of the French doors on his way through, they rattle in response.

CHAPTER 26

Beatrice

I wake up but don't open my eyes. It's the morning I go home and I want to stay in bed, think about last night and relive images of Benedict and his hot body as we made love. I can feel his delicious warmth next to me, a solid presence of libidinous man, I turn my head in his direction, open one eye and take a peak.

'Morning beautiful! Sleep well?'

Damn he beat me to it.

He is grinning at me, his dimples looking sexy along with his messy bed hair. He springs up and over me, tenting the duvet above us and leans on his elbows. 'You are definitely my new favourite sight in the morning' he gives me a peck on the lips 'I enjoyed watching you sleep, your eyelashes were fluttering adorably ... were you dreaming about me?' he nestles himself between my legs and I can feel the stirrings of an erection. He raises his eyebrows playfully.

'You're in a good mood this morning.' I tease

'That's because I have woken up with you and now you can't escape!' he grinds his hips into me and holds me vice like with his forearms. I squeal, my restricted position turns me on and my core clenches delectably. He drops his head and our lips are just about to kiss, I feel the familiar magnetic pull as my senses anticipate the exquisite sensation of his touch.

Bang! Bang! Bang! Three loud knocks on the door interrupt our foreplay.

'Ugh bloody hell what now' says Benedict grumpily climbing off me

'What shall I do?' I whisper hastily, aware that 'we' are still a secret

'Wait there and don't move.' He gets out of bed shouting 'Hang on!' as he grabs some sweats and is pulling them on as the door opens from the outside. I flip the duvet over my head in a futile attempt not to get caught and Benedict manages to get to the door before whoever it is makes it fully into the bedroom.

To my surprise I hear Ursula's voice. 'Hi Benedict, sorry to disturb you, I have been looking everywhere for Beatrice and she is not in her room or downstairs. You haven't seen her have you?'

'No, not yet' he lies on our behalf 'shall I give her a message if I do see her'

'That'll be great, it was just that Holly needs her, I'll keep looking .... Thank you!' And she disappears.

He closes the door and I flap the duvet back, my face red from being covered 'Phew that was close!'

'She so didn't believe me, she was trying to look over my shoulder, convinced you were in here!' Benedict turns back looking devilish and is about to leap back into bed 'Anyway where were we'

'You can't' I bemoan sitting up and jumping out 'I've got to get up we're all supposed to be leaving soon.' I hunt around for my things I don't have any clothes on.

'I'm going to have blue balls again all day thinking of you like this' he whines and I spot his erection tenting inside his sweat pants.

I shove on my clothes hastily and give him a kiss on the lips, he groans again 'This isn't helping!'

'You need to see me out, I've got to get to my bedroom without being spotted.'

Reluctantly, he takes my hand and leads me to the door, opens it and peers around.

'All quiet out here' he whispers and I make my escape.

I shower in my bedroom and shove my clothes and toiletries into my bag ready to leave when needed. I didn't realise how late it was and have missed the breakfast, no wonder people wondered where I was. I leave my things in my room and go out in search of Holly.

She is still in her bedroom and in a dressing gown when I knock on her door.

'Beatrice, just the person' she says as I enter 'Ursula has been looking everywhere for you, are you ok?'

'Yes fine, I have just seen Benedict and he told me you were both looking for me' I don't want to lie totally just twist the truth a little for now.

'I am sorry' she starts 'I didn't get a chance to talk to you about this yesterday, you went to bed early after supper.'

'Sorry yes I was tired'

'Bit of a last minute arrangement I hope you don't mind but Claud asked me yesterday if I would like to travel back to London with him and he will drop me home. I know that means you will be driving alone.' She looks at me with a wry expression and tentatively hedges 'or maybe you could suggest to Benedict that he comes with you so you are not on your own .... you know perhaps settle your differences?' Looking at me pointedly she raises her eyebrows, I know that she knows more than she is letting on. I play ignorant.

'For you cousin, anything, I know you would appreciate some alone time with Claud and I can dutifully save Benedict from being a gooseberry.' The thought of a couple of hours of banter in the car with Benedict quite appealing.

Her face lights up 'love you so much' she gives me a hug 'now help me, I can't decide what to wear for this all important car trip.' Gesturing to some clothes laid out on the bed 'Yellow dress or khaki shorts?'

'Both lovely but go with khaki shorts – more casual'

'Hmm not sure I was thinking yellow dress, more feminine'

'Up to you'

'But I can't make a decision' she moans

'Go shorts'

'I think I'm going to go dress' she holds it up

'Perfect I say – actually that does look gorgeous, lucky Claud won't be able to keep his hands off you.'

'That's what I am hoping!' she giggles.

'I'm so happy and excited for you' I turn to go 'see you downstairs, I'll get my car packed up with my stuff and we can say our goodbye's outside.'

I grab my bag from my room and make my way down the front stairs.

Everyone is mingling in the front hall. I can't see Conrad or Boris and wonder if they have already left. Leo and Inno are chatting to Pete and John who look like they are on the point of leaving.

Holly joins me as I reach the bottom of the stairs, she is buzzing with the excitement of her impending car journey as she bounds up to her parents. I am behind her as Claud comes over looking uncharacteristically serious, his gaze to the floor, Benedict is behind him looking concerned. He catches my eye and I see a ghost of a smile cross his face.

Leo beckons to Claud 'I gather you are going to kindly give a lift to my daughter.'

'No' he says simply

Benedict interjects 'Ha he's teasing' and elbows Claud looking sternly at him.

Leo looks a little confused and turns to Holly 'All set? I thought you're going with Claud aren't you?'

'I am' says Holly but she suddenly looks unsure, there appears to be a tension between the men which we can now all sense.

Claud looks up and accusingly at Holly 'Is there any reason why I might not want to take you in my car?'

Holly is stunned, as we all are, Claud is behaving really oddly. 'None at all that I can think of' she says looking confused.

Pete meanwhile has come over and speaks up 'Claud has seen otherwise, in fact a few of us did last night.'

'I did indeed' he lets forth 'I no longer have any interest in taking you in my car or seeing you further.' Poor Holly gasps in horror and feels for and grasps my hand. 'You see I saw what you were up to last night, it seems it wasn't just me who you wanted to play around with and now you want to make me look like a fool!'

Leo jumping to the defence of Holly. 'What on earth are you talking about man? Do you have any proof?'

Claud barrels on 'I saw with my own eyes, as did Pete and John. Tell me. Who were you with at your bedroom window last night?'

'I don't know what you are talking about!' stammers Holly 'I wasn't with anyone, I was on my own!'

Claud continues 'That's not what we saw' and turning to Leo 'It seems your daughter has developed a taste for more than just one of the regiment!'

John turns to Holly 'I saw you first, and didn't believe it was true either, so I went to get Pete and Claud. We saw what was going on, all three of us couldn't have been imagining it.'

Poor Holly looks in horror at the sea of faces regarding her accusingly, it's as if she has been indicted for witch craft. My blood is about of boil over at Claud's ridiculous insinuations.

'I don't believe it! It's not true!' she pleads and with a cry turns to flee back up the stairs.

It's awful, everyone has gone quiet in the hall, just staring in shock at Holly's departing back. I am absolutely furious, I don't know what they are all talking about, but my first priority is with Holly so I turn, giving all the men a filthy look, and climb back up the stairs to find her distraught in her bedroom.

She is sitting on the edge of her bed crying angry tears. I sit down next to her and put my arm around her shoulders.
'That was hideous, I didn't know what to do! What do you think I am supposed to have done?' Her fists thump against her thighs in hopeless frustration. 'I hate Claud, he has embarrassed me in front of everyone, not least my parents. I never want to see him again!'

'He is such a stupid wanker' I say in my fury of him 'obviously there has been some huge misunderstanding but he didn't even have the wit to try to find out from you what has happened. I'll go back down and try to find out what is going on. Will you be ok until I come back?'

'Yes go'

'I'll come back up as soon as I find anything out, have a glass of water' I poor some from the jug on her bedside table and hand the glass to her 'if you are ok I'll go' as I get to the door I turn around one last time to check she is ok 'I'll be as quick as I can' I say before shutting her door behind me.

When I get back downstairs I find that Pete, John and Claud have already left. Claud didn't take Benedict with him, he is still standing with Leo and Inno, there is a tense atmosphere.

Benedict as soon as he sees me asks 'Is she ok?'

'Not really no, thanks to Claud, what on earth has gotten into him?'

'I gather the boys caught Holly with Boris last night.' Leo speaks 'Claud is really upset. I must admit I am pretty cross with her myself. It doesn't look good that the Colonel of the regiment's daughter is fooling around with more than one of its members.'

'There must be an explanation.' Benedict says 'let's not jump to conclusions just yet.'

'She has been so wronged.' I say 'Come on you all know Holly and know that she would never have done this. She had genuine feelings for Claud, why on earth would she mess around with Boris, of all people? I mean no offence, but really?' I look pointedly at Leo to try to impress on him the ridiculousness of it all. 'There is not a bad bone in her body and I am surprised that Claud, who I thought was totally infatuated with her, couldn't see that or wait to find a logical explanation.'

'They did seem so convinced at what they saw, but they had been drinking' muses Benedict 'I have a hunch that they have been subjected to a nasty prank somehow. I wouldn't be at all surprised if John isn't behind this. He's done it before and revels is causing and creating dramas.'

'Well I don't know what to make of it' says Leo

'We need time to find out what has gone on' an idea forms in my mind 'Let's make out that Holly was so traumatised by Claud's accusation that she is suffering a bout of depression, and ill, taken to her bed.'

'And how will that help?' asks Leo

'Rather than everyone accusing Holly and thinking badly of her they will feel sorry for her that she has been taken so ill and in doing so stop the gossip mill in its tracks.'

'And I will get to the bottom of what the boys think they saw, find out what has really gone on and deal with them appropriately.' Benedict says resolutely

'This seems a very sensible approach' Inno, who has been quietly observing the whole charade, now speaks up. 'I'm grateful to you both' turning to her husband 'Come on I'll put the kettle on let's have a coffee' she puts her arm around Leo and leads him to the kitchen. Ursula and my father, who have been wisely keeping in the background, follow them.

Benedict stays behind in the hall with me. 'Are you ok?'

'I will be once all this is sorted'

'I don't like thinking of you sad'

'It's not your fault'

'For what it's worth I do think your cousin has been wrongly accused.'

'I know she has and I will do anything for the person who proves it'

'And I will do anything to try to make you happy. You know how I feel about you don't you? I like you, an awful lot in fact, I want us to be an "Us". And for us see a lot more of each other after this weekend....' His hands are on my shoulders and he looks earnestly into my eyes.

'Knowing what I was like before this weekend do you find that strange?' he questions as if he has asked himself the same thing and doesn't know the answer.

'Very, and you were in no doubt of what I thought of you, so the fact that I like you a lot in return, you must find it strange too?' I don't know the answer either.

'Anyway I am sad for Holly.' I say

Benedict is still thinking about my previous sentence 'I love that you like me too' he smiles

'I do and you know it! But for god's sake...'

'What? Tell me what I can do for you. I'll do anything' his smile turns to an imploring look.

'Kill Claud!'

'That's a bit extreme!'

I don't mean it literally, although I am bloody furious with the way he has treated Holly, I'm kind of testing his reaction 'Well if you're going to go so quickly back on your word we are done here' I turn to walk back up the stairs but he grasps my arm.

'Hang on not so fast' I hear a little panic in his voice.

'I must go and see if Holly is ok'

'Please just talk a bit longer I don't want you to rush off on unfriendly terms.'

'I am just so frustrated that there is nothing I can do. I wasn't there last night because I was in your room. It is the one evening I could have been around for Holly, to be her alibi and prove she wasn't with Boris and that is what makes me so cross with myself. The chance for me to be a real friend and I was up to the one thing I swore I would never do. Leo is worried about her' I use my fingers to indicate speech marks "reputation" 'or more importantly to him, his. I cannot believe in this day and age it is poor Holly who is supposed to be at fault and not Boris who gets away blameless .... Where is he, by the way, surely he should be partially accountable for what has gone on?'

'That is exactly where I intend to start, nobody has seen Conrad or Boris this morning. It appears they have left without saying good bye which is odd.'

'I wonder if Megan knows anything, I haven't seen her either' it suddenly occurs to me.

'You know your cousin is innocent, go and comfort her' he orders 'I will keep my word, make my enquiries to find out what really happened, spreading the word that Holly is suffering from depression and has become bed bound. I'll see you later on' He kisses me on the lips, then kisses again, groaning in anguish at pulling away he leaves me as I climb back up the stairs in search of Holly.

CHAPTER 27

Benedict

I walk through to the kitchen, Leo, Tony, Inno and Ursula are sitting round the table looking glum.

'Don't beat yourself up over this' Tony says to Leo

'I can't help it' says Leo 'I am cross with Holly because she has brought this upon her head and I am cross with Claud for embarrassing her and making such a public display of it. And the most frustrating thing is I can't do anything about it.'

'Well then you do need to do something about it otherwise it will just eat away at you.' Tony says 'What does your hunch tell you?'

'That there has been a big mistake somewhere and I think Beatrice is right, I don't think Holly would do what they think she has because she is like her mother and loyalty is important to her. The only thing we can do is make sure Claud knows that.'

Inno looks up at me standing by the table 'Coffee Benedict?'

'No but thank you I'm going to head out and try to come up with a plan of action. I'll let you know if I hear anything'

I leave the kitchen and make my way outside, walking round to the front of the house to seek better mobile reception. My first port of call is to find out from Pete what the hell is going on.

'Hi mate' he answers after a few rings

'Well you have all certainly caused a commotion here, where are you?'

'We only got as far as The White Hart in the middle of the village, enjoying a midday beer and consoling Claud. Come and join us, he needs some cheering up'

'Ok how do I find you?'

'It's less than half a mile away, I think there is a short cut on a footpath from the back of the house.... hang on.....yup ok I get it ..... thanks mate ...... barman says follow the footpath till you meet a back lane, turn left and after about fifty metres turn right and you will see the pub across the road on the right.'

'I know the one, shouldn't take long, see you in 15'

I hang up and double back up to the stile behind the tennis court, the one I went for a run from yesterday, marvelling at how much my world has turned around in the course of the last twenty four hours. I pretty much knew the way Pete was describing, as I had found the lane yesterday, but for something to do while I am walking there I open up my running app and map my route to find the pub.

Even though it is a sunny day and there are tables outside Pete and Claud are sitting indoors. The light is dull inside, it is a classic old style drinker's pub with a dark oak bar and dark wood tables chairs and benches. Beams run across the ceiling and down the walls, horse brasses hang off them in vertical rows interspersed with old fashioned hunting pictures.

'Brilliant just the man.' Pete welcomes me as I enter 'What can I get you? There is a good local ale "Northern Lights" which we are sampling.' They already have two empty glasses on the table so must be on their second pints.

More than sampling I think to myself 'Sounds good I'll have one of those, thanks'

He gestures to the barman and orders me a pint.

'What's happening at the house?' Claud speaks up for the first time.

'Did we leave the two old boys spitting out their false teeth over our discovery?' Pete says laughing

'Actually not funny, I came to find you both, we need to talk.' and turning to Claud 'You have been a prize dick.'

'That's rich coming from you, pot and kettle and all that.' Pete tries to defend him. 'Poor Claud thought he had found the love of his life, only for her to shove it back in his face and get off with Boris.'

'Either that or maybe he's joking with us' Claud says 'ha very funny Ben – but that's not the best way to cheer me up.'

'Thanks' I say to the barman and take a sip of the beer which has just been put in front of me, it is surprisingly smooth. 'I'm not joking, you jumped to conclusions without talking to Holly first. She is distraught, I left the house with her in bed suffering the onset of depression. This is on your head.' Claud shakes his head at me 'Come on she is a sweet girl' I try to appeal to his reason 'and doesn't deserve your treatment of her, surely from the short time you have known her you can see she wouldn't have behaved in the way you have accused her. You are a coward in shaming her so publicly, you know that don't you?'

Pete sits back in his chair and squints his eyes at me for effect. 'Do you know what I think?' They are not taking me seriously, two pints of beer not helping. 'I think you have come straight from Beatrice, this sounds like her speaking, you're in love Mountant, are you her lackey now doing just what you've been told to do?'

Oh bloody hell!

'You're right!' Claud sits up gleefully and joins in 'he's definitely a changed man, busted Mountant, this is much more entertaining!'

I need to change the subject. Taking a sip of my beer and ignoring their taunts, something occurs to me 'Where's John by the way?'

That stops them in their tracks and they have the decency to look sheepish.

'He said something had come up and he had to leave urgently.' Pete says 'He took my car as Claud is going to give me a lift back, seeing as he won't be taking Holly now.'

'Doesn't that strike you as suspicious, knowing your brother?' I question

'That's not fair, he's got much better these days.' His voice trails off, I think Pete is trying to convince himself as well as us of that one.

We fall silent and drink our beer in contemplation. Presently two older men come into the pub. One very tall and the other much shorter. They look a bit dishevelled and the shorter one is doing all the talking.

'Mornin' Simon' he says to the barman 'Lovely day, too nice to be sittin' indoors.' He looks explicitly at us, he has a point. 'Morning' he nods in our direction 'or afternoon I think it is now'. We lift our glasses and nod in response.

'What can I get you gentlemen?' the barman asks them.

'Two halves of your finest Scrumpy please, firsty work this neighbourhood watch business.'

They take their cider and turn around, the shorter one is looking towards us. We're not talking so he takes his cue to say something.

'You're not local are you? Been staying with the party up at the 'all?' He has a regional accent and addresses us in a slightly accusing way.

'Yes we have' I reply trying to be friendly 'Leo's the colonel of our regiment, we've been staying as his guests since before the ball.'

The other taller man shuffles and grunts but doesn't say anything. 'Hmmmm' says the shorter one 'very nice I'm sure .... anyway we'll leave you gentl'men to it, enjoy the rest of your so jorn.'

Claud sniggers rudely, but I think they're trying to be friendly, they just get it a bit wrong. They take their drinks outside and sit at the table by the open front door. We can't help but overhear them talking because the shorter one has a loud voice and seems to like the sound of it. They are discussing or rather he is regaling his account of his patrol of the village last night. He sounds like an old fashioned comedy policeman, he speaks using factual words but keeps saying them incorrectly.

'how bout you Vince, anything to report?'

'Not much just a couple of young lads, think they m'been stayin' at th'all too' our ears all prick up at this. 'They was sittin' against one of them grave stones at th 'all chapel when I was patrollin' the grounds. Must've bin about two aye em. One o them was cryin'

'Did you over hear anythin' signifificant?' the shorter one asks

'I didn't min to eavesdrop but I needed to make sure they wasn't up t'no good'

'Go on'

'Well he was cryin' bout being cheated n stuff, somthin' bout his boyfriend who is not his boyfriend anymore'

'Well there you go then' says the shorter one 'now't so queer as folk' then he laughs but the taller one doesn't react 'ha ha get it?' the taller one still doesn't react so the shorter one coughs to clear his throat 'anythin' else?'

The three of us stay silent, glued to what the men are saying.

'Well the other one seemed really cross and said somthin' bout them both being cheated coz he was supposed to be paid for somthin' he did with a girl to make it look like it was with another girl. He was talkin' bout Megan, who works with the 'orses' uppat th'all. Anyways the'didn't appear t'be causing no trouble so I left 'em to it.'

I look back to Claud and Pete who look as stunned as I am at what we have overheard.

'That has made my blood run cold' Pete speaks first

'I feel sick' is all Claud can say

'I knew your brother was behind it' I add

'And not only that, true to form he has scarpered while everyone else will be left to pick up the pieces' Pete looks more upset than angry 'Sounds like he has also done the dirty on Conrad too, who really liked him. God what an awful situation poor Conrad'll never trust another man again.'

'I have been such a fool! Oh God Holly I am so sorry!' Claud groans putting his head in his hands.

I rise from my seat and go out the door to the two men.

'I'm sorry' I say to them 'I couldn't help overhearing what you just said'

The shorter one stands up 'I'm Dave' he sticks his hand out to me which I shake 'this is Vince, we head up the neighbourhood watch program in the village'

'Then the village is in safe hands' I say and Dave visibly puffs his chest out. 'I think you have overheard something important which the Colonel would be very interested to hear about.'

'Is that right?' says Dave

'Is there any chance you would go and tell your account of last night up at the hall?'

'If you think it is important then of course we will' he downs the rest of his cider 'come on Vince our work isn't done yet.' Vince downs his drink too and they both stand up 'We'll be seein' you' he says to me and they walk back up the road that I had just come down.

CHAPTER 28

Beatrice

'Beatrice! Holly!' Inno is shouting up the stairs to us 'Come down!' Then Ursula bursts into our room.

'You've got to come down!' she exclaims 'There's a mega hubbub going on in the kitchen. Those two funny men are there'

'Oh not them' says Holly 'they're the last thing I need, can you go Bea?'

'No you must come' Ursula urges 'they have proof that you were falsely accused of whatever last night. Pete and Claud have been made fools of and John is behind it all!'

'Come on Hol lets go and hear them out' I encourage.

Down in the kitchen we listen to Dave's confusing account of what Vince had overheard. Inno is making a big fuss of them and Dave is purple with pride as he is the one to deliver the news of Vince's discovery.

'Thank you gentlemen' Leo says 'I am beyond grateful you have taken the trouble to come and tell us this.'

'Any time sir' Dave says

Leo hands them some cash 'A couple of pints at the White Hart on me' he says

'Thank you that's much depreciated. Well best beon our way.'

As they leave we hear the crunching sound of car tires arriving on the gravel out front.

Leo speaks up 'Well if that's Claud and Pete I want to have a word with them. Holly make yourself scarce, I have an idea and you must still be bed bound.'

I see Holly out to the bottom of the stairs, she turns to me 'That'll teach me not to make fun of Dave and Vince in future, I have a lot to thank them for' she says earnestly. 'God what a mess, I kind of feel sorry for Claud, he's been made to look stupid and now he's got to face my father!'

'He'll get over it, it's a good life lesson'

'I'd better go' Holly disappears up the back stairs as the door opens at the front of the house.

CHAPTER 29

Benedict

Leo opens the door to the three of us 'Here they are' He announces, in a rather unamused way.

Claud moves forward to Leo 'I have to speak first. I am truly sorry, I feel extremely stupid and have caused so much harm to you and your family, especially as you had welcomed us so generously into your home. I know I have been a gullible fool, I had drunk too much and too readily believed what John was telling me.'

'And me too' says Pete stepping forward to join them 'I feel partially responsible, I thought my brother had changed for the better and I wanted to believe that he was being honest. I realise now that he has tricked us all'

'I am grateful you have had had the courage to face me to apologise' Leo says 'You can't undo the damage that has been done, my daughter is not very well and I don't know how long it will take her to recover.' Claud hangs his head in shame, I feel for him. 'I think the best course of action is to go back to London and take some time to think about what has happened. I believe you have a week off further and then you are bound for Herefordshire?' They both nod. 'If I am right you will next have leave in three weeks from then. By then if, and only if, my daughter is well enough and still wants to see you, you can apologise to her face to face then.'

I see the relief in Claud's face 'Thank you so much, you have been incredibly understanding' ... bless him 'I will pray every day for her swift recovery. A month it is.' He turns to go.

Pete shakes Leo's hand. 'I can't thank you enough or apologise enough.'

'Well let's hope there is no serious harm done. I'm coming to visit you all in Herefordshire in a couple of weeks so until then.' He turns back towards the house and talking to himself he mutters 'In the meantime I need to find Megan and have a word with her' and disappears through the front door.

'Are you going to come with us?' Claud asks me

'I'm good thank you – I'll keep my promise and go back with Beatrice, so she is not driving on her own as I assume Holly will stay here.'

'Very thoughtful' he says patting me patronisingly on the shoulder 'We'll catch up next week?'

'Yes sure I'll give you a call' I say as they climb into the front seats of the range rover. Churning up gravel they disappear back down the drive.

Turning back to the house I see Beatrice standing in the doorway.

'God what a day.' I say as I reach her, looking around to confirm we are on our own 'I missed you' I whisper as I bend my head down to kiss her. She crinkles her nose.

'Eeeew beer breath! Have you been enjoying yourself rather too much at the pub?' she asks and before I answer 'Well you'll have to suffer and wait till later, then you can kiss me!'

I groan 'Oh I do suffer believe me, and will suffer till later. Give me something to keep me going then, tell me about all of my bad bits, the ones which most appealed to you and made you realise you had feelings for me?'

'There's too many to mention' she puts her head on one side looking skyward as if thinking hard, 'so many there is no room for the good ones' she is enjoying this 'better still tell me about all of my good bits, the ones that made you fall for me?'

Shaking my head I say forlornly 'I fell for you against my will' she looks at me in mock horror. 'I had no say in the matter' I go on 'it was my heart and body that couldn't help themselves. If my wise mind had any say in the matter it would have left well alone'

'Real wise men do not claim themselves to be so therefore you are not as you claim'

'Right for that you will have to endure my beer breath' she shrieks as I pull her to me and slam my mouth on to her, protesting loudly her noises turns from shrieks to a hum and then she gives in kissing me back. *Hmmmm* her ambrosial lips feel so soft against mine, a delicious frisson flows between us, the sensation pure heaven. I pull away and look into her eyes 'God you're gorgeous' she smiles and her turquoise eyes catch the sunlight and sparkle, it takes my breath away and for a moment I stare in wonder, marvelling at every aspect of her stunning face, in awe of her natural beauty.

I am so done for.

CHAPTER 30

Benedict

The next few weeks pass by so slowly. I had managed to see Beatrice during my week off in London, but as she had said she would be, was tied up with work. She gets to the office ridiculously early and doesn't finish until well into the night. I only managed to see her at her flat when she finally got home late a couple of times. I stayed, but she was exhausted and I had to make do with a takeaway to catch up over, then cuddling her in bed, my face buried in the back of her neck and my body buzzing with unrequited sexual need while she breathed deeply asleep.

It hasn't diminished my feelings for her, if anything they have gotten stronger, they say absence makes the heart grow fonder which is more than applicable in my case. The frustrating thing, being base in Herefordshire, for our first three weeks we have exercise and training over the weekends so I can't get to London to see Beatrice when she would normally be free. We speak on our mobiles, reception is crap here though so even that can be a frustrating few minutes of missed words and robotic sounding voices. With the goal in mind of our planned weekend and I am finally allowed to escape, Beatrice is going to work Saturdays and Sundays until then, to try to get ahead herself . I can't wait to enjoy a full two days together without needing to fret about getting other stuff done.

Claud is mooning about Holly, we make quite a pair, even

though he doesn't know this. He hasn't pushed me about my feelings for Beatrice but it is harder for him as he is suffering the four weeks with no contact at all, not knowing how he is going to be received. It must feel a long time when you don't know whether the person you want to have a relationship with will still feel the same about you or hate your guts for being treated so badly. He is keeping to his word and giving her the space he was asked to do, I know he feels guilty for being such an idiot. He knows she is worth the wait, his feelings are strong. I would be the same if I were in his position, knowing that Beatrice is more than worth the wait.

Poor Conrad, has had his heart well and truly broken. It must have been hard for him knowing he was gay and having to deal with that reality on his own, especially within such a testosterone fuelled environment as the army. To have been deceived by John, his first proper partnering, must be detrimental to his self-esteem. I have tried to talk to him, but I'm not the best person to give council, especially given its subject matter. All I can do is listen, he is finding it hard to talk but I will give him the space he needs, knowing he will come to me when he is ready.

Frustrated at not being able to talk properly to Beatrice either via phone or text I try to email her. Unusual for me, I am not the best of writers but my hopeless attempts at trying to express my feelings are in vain as I leave every version in my draft folder in the hope I will get it right tomorrow, but I never do. My biggest fear is that to her I will be 'out of sight out of mind' and I really don't want her to lose interest in me. It's a constant cause of anxiety among my friends, who like me, in the first tentative months of a relationship have to endure weeks of absence. Charlotte was proof to that and memories of her aren't helping.

Some good news is that I am up for promotion to Major. I have been in the army for over eight years and earned the slightly early advance. I will be given command of a sub unit of 120 soldiers and officers, looking after their training and welfare and leading them on operations. Being mentored by Leo has definitely helped me to prepare for this next step and I am looking forward to being challenged again.

CHAPTER 31

Beatrice

Finally our first weekend together arrives, it feels like it's been a long three weeks with contact sketchy, hampered by bad lines and impersonal texts that can't convey what we really want to say. Thankfully I have been able to bury my head in work, I have been overwhelmed with our new case and focusing on that has kept my mind busy and not able to dwell on thoughts of Benedict for too long.

I don't want to wait to meet him somewhere formal so am going to his flat after work, via home to pick up my car and change out of work clothes. We should arrive at a similar time as he will have been driving himself back from Herefordshire. I learnt, when we had time to really talk on our return trip from the Uppaugh's, that he is a biker. The thought of him having an accident is terrifying, bikes can be dangerous, vulnerable to inattentive motorists, so I wasn't delighted by that discovery. He proudly told me he has a Triumph Speed Triple which didn't mean much to me but I was shown his pride and joy when I dropped him home. It does looks cool with its classic Triumph embossing and sleek black and silver chassis but anything to do with torque or performance is way out of my scope of knowledge.

When I draw up outside his flat I can't see his bike anywhere so assume he hasn't arrived back yet. Managing to find a parking spot not far away I take the opportunity to take a breath, lean my chair back, relax and flip through my phone.

We are going to meet Claud and Holly for lunch tomorrow. She has forgiven him, but he doesn't know that yet, no harm in making him suffer after what he did to her. She knows now that he is easily lead and that John, who is jealous of anyone's happiness, took advantage of his. John is such a jerk leading on Conrad in the way he did, all for some stupid prank. I hope he has seen that it has backfired on him too and he goes someway to realising what he has lost for himself in the process.

Holly is excited and nervous about seeing Claud, they are having dinner together on their own this evening, it will be his opportunity to grovel his way back into her favour and time for them to rekindle what was snatched away from them four weeks ago.

The roar of a motorbike interrupts my thoughts as a shadow crosses and stops in my side window. I look up to see Benedict flip up his visor and those familiar blue eyes smile at me from inside his helmet. He gestures to a space he will park his bike and as he moves into it I grab my bag and climb out of my car.

I am unprepared for the panty dropping sight of Benedict head to toe in black leather.

Jesus Fucking Christ!

He dismounts from his bike and takes off his helmet and balaclava shaking his hair and pushing it back to unstick it from around his head. He looks imposing and so sexy, his formidable body filling out his jacket and his thighs shapely inside the trousers. My mind flicks through fantasy scenarios, like a silent film noir, as I rush up to him and into an all-consuming hug breathing in the scent of leather, which creaks softly as he throws his arms around me.

'God I've missed you!' he says

I had forgotten his sheer presence, he is all man and muscle and makes me feel petit and womanly, not the heavy shapely oaf I usually think of myself. I realise how much I've missed him too.

'It is so good to see you' I say just before his lips land on mine, the first intimate contact in reacquainting ourselves since our separation, we kiss in the street, relieved we are finally together.

'Let's go in before I ravish you out here' he takes his rucksack off flinging it over his shoulder as we enter his apartment building. It's a newly built block, four storeys high with a cream stone façade and oblong tall black framed windows. There are two shops along the ground floor, a coffee shop and florists with the entrance in between. We enter the functional entrance lobby, encasing us with its beige marble walls and floor and Benedict calls for the lift as his apartment is on the fourth floor. We hold hands to maintain contact, and as we ride the lift and arrive at his apartment he talks me through briefly what he has been up to over the last couple of days.

Ushering me in first, I take a look around, it's a very modern space almost all one big room divided into areas by a free standing wall which stands across the middle. Along one side there are kitchen units which face a long island, bar stools line up along the far length of this and beyond them a chunky wooden dining table surrounded by retro 1950's style chairs. At the far end of the room is one deep long sofa and a couple of single armchairs which look towards a huge flat screen wall TV, it's a real 'lad's' apartment.

'Make yourself at home' he tells me. 'I need to get out of my leathers and take a quick shower. There is some wine in the fridge, or beer, so do help yourself.'

'Can I get you anything too?'

'Beer please, there is an opener in the drawer opposite.'

I select a bottle of Italian white I hadn't heard of before called Fiano and busy myself opening it. I find a glass for myself and open a beer for Benedict. The wine is delicious, pale straw in colour with a honey nutty taste, unlike anything I have had before. I enjoy a few sips then take my glass and go for a wander. Behind the wall are two bedrooms with a bathroom in the middle, Benedict is currently showering with the door open. Forcing myself not to take a peek inside, I move on to have a look at the bedrooms. One of the rooms, which must be the spare one, is small with a double bed in the middle taking up most of the room. The second bedroom is much bigger and the bed in the middle is enormous. *I wouldn't have expected anything less.* There are bedside tables on either side and a bank of fitted mirrored wardrobes covering the facing wall. The décor in both rooms is in complimenting shades of grey and black, very male in taste. It looks like there has been a professional hand involved in putting it all together.

Benedict comes out of the bathroom with just a towel slung around his hips the steam billowing around him like a contestant in a before and after show. There are water droplets all over his ripped chest, another vision I had forgotten quite how fabulous, and his hair is slicked back wet from the shower. My eyes follow the beautiful contours across his torso and round each bicep, to stop myself literally disappearing in a pool of hormones on the floor I have to take a sip of wine. Drawing my lower lip into my mouth to lick off a stray droplet I check myself from so obviously gawping by turning round to pick up his beer, which I hand to him.

'Great thanks' he takes a mouthful, his eyes on my lips. The doorbell rings 'Good, perfect timing' Benedict goes to the intercom 'Hi can you bring it up to my apartment, number 15 on the fourth floor?' and then turning to me by way of explanation 'food delivery, I have nothing in the flat, I thought we could eat in tonight, hope that's ok.'

He seems totally unbothered letting in the delivery guy, wrapped in just a towel, and the bags are dutifully dumped on the island before he finds his wallet in his leather trousers, tips the man and we are left alone again.

'You can't just stand there in nothing but your towel and expect me to concentrate on eating' I say

He raises an eyebrow cheekily at me 'Oh did you have something in mind?'

'You know what I mean' I say blushing.

He acquiesces, returning to his bedroom to find some sweatpants. Pulling them up as he walks back out, he says 'I've spent the last three weeks anticipating and imagining this evening, planning all the things I want to do to you, us to do together, so you'll have to be patient. We have all night and I fully intend to make it one to remember.'

He steps closer to me, looking into my eyes, and plants the gentlest kiss on my lips. The feeling takes my breath away, my lips tingling from his touch.

'Ugh' he moans 'that just makes me want to fling you over my shoulder and take you to bed now! Come on lets have something to eat before I do just that'.

He starts to unpack the shopping delivery

'What can I do?' I ask

He pulls out the cutlery drawer 'knives and forks in here' then indicating to another drawer with his foot 'mats and plates in here. You have a wine glass, grab a water one if you like. Are you ok with sushi?'

'Love it, yes please' it's a perfect choice not too filling or bloating which is helpful as I have a feeling I might be taking off my clothes afterwards.

'Good. Can you grab the candle, it's over there on the sideboard.' He points to a low cupboard next to the sofas, pulls out another drawer and hands me a lighter.

I complete my tasks while Benedict puts groceries from the bags into the fridge and lays out prepared sushi. Taking a seat at the island when I am done, I sip my wine and watch him at work.

'How's Claud?' I ask

'Good, excited and nervous, I think. He's been fretting about meeting Holly for the last month. I assume things will be ok between them or you would have said something earlier. Please tell me she is not about to break his heart?'

'She's not, she forgave him almost as soon as he came to apologise to her father. But Leo wanted him to learn a lesson for reacting too hastily, especially as it was to the detriment of his darling daughter, so Holly has respectfully adhered to her father's wishes too.'

'Thank God for that, well hopefully lunch tomorrow will be a whole lot more fun for all of us.' Benedict picks up his phone and after tapping on the screen chilled music starts to play throughout the apartment. 'Do you like Lauv?'

'Sure, sounds good'

He lays out plates of sushi and sauce on the table. 'Let's eat, I'm starving after three hours on a bike.'

'Don't you stop and take a break?'

He pulls out a chair for me to sit on 'Not when I have a beautiful red head waiting for me at the other end' Moving round the narrow table he sits opposite me and reaches his legs out, hooking them around mine so that they are interlocked. I look up at him 'It's good to stay connected.' He smiles.

'This sushi is awesome' he says. Picking up a salmon wrap expertly in his chopsticks he dips it in the horseradish and offers it to my mouth. 'Try it, more fun feeding each other.'

'Ok' I lean forward and take it all in my mouth. It's delicious but the sauce goes straight to my sinus and makes my eyes water. 'Wow!' is all I can say as Benedict chuckles seeing the effect it has on me.

'Whoops sorry too much sauce?' he says cheekily

So he wants to play dirty hmm? 'My turn' I squeak once I can speak and breath after the last mouthful. I pick up my chopsticks and select a piece of the ginger and a salmon roll and make sure it is dunked deeply into the horseradish, offering it to Benedict.

'Oh God' he says before taking the mouthful.

I take pleasure in his wincing as the sauce has the same effect on him and his eyes water, making them sparkle more.

'Ok we're definitely even.' Benedict says hoarsely, holding his hand up, he selects the next piece, this time dipping it lightly 'Ginger?'

'No thanks – don't think I could take any more heat.' He feeds me an avocado one which is perfect on its balance of taste and spice.

We continue our little game of feeding each other until I am full and can't eat anymore. Benedict asks me about my work in-between mouthfuls, although there is some stuff I can't talk about he shows real interest asking lots of questions and I enjoy talking about it. He finishes the remainder sushi, managing to consume more than double I did, then leaping out of his chair, before I get the chance, he takes the plates away and putting them in the dishwasher he asks 'Pudding?'

'Something small, I'm stuffed' I say not thinking about the connotations.

'Not yet you're not.' He retorts with a wry smile

I look at him incredulously 'Really? Is that the best you can come up with?'

'What can I say?' he busies himself loading more things onto plates and putting something in the microwave. My mouth waters as the plates get laid out on the table, strawberries, cherries, melted chocolate, marshmallows, ice cream and amoretti biscuits, some of my favourite things. Without thinking I select a cherry, dangling it above my lips by its stalk, my tongue reaches out and draws it into my mouth. Benedict has stilled on his way to sit down and watches me. He waits till I have spat out the stone.

'Ugh I give in' he says, in a flash he is round to my side of the table, lifts me off my feet and kisses me with such a force, for a moment I am taken back, then as the familiar sparks ignite between us, I match his ardour, our tongues and teeth clashing in the urgent need to have more of each other. My top is lifted over my head and I push down my floaty summer skirt and stamp on it to remove it. Our tongues still warring he reaches round and unclips my bra, as my breasts are released he clasps me to him skin to skin. His body is warm and I can feel the faster beating of his heart across my chest, I inhale his clean body smell and the aroma of the shower gel along with his unique yummy deliciousness.

'Hmmm so good.' I say

'Come on lets have some fun.' He says lifting me up, I shriek in surprise.

Throwing me over his shoulder, in a fireman's life, still in my panties and shoes he stalks us to the sofa, I scream 'put me down!' and receive two sharp smacks to my bottom. 'Ow!' I squeal as he massages away the sting and heat swarms to the area. He grabs a cushion and trots us back, putting the cushion on the table and seating me on it. 'Such a gentleman' I say, somewhat sarcastically.

He plants my feet on two chairs with my legs apart making me more vulnerable and at his mercy, and says, his voice deep. 'Careful I'm the one in charge now. You know the punishment.'

My body reacts and I pulse between my legs feeling the excitement twist inside me at his domineering tone.

'Dessert' he says simply then more demanding 'put your hands behind you on the table and lean back'. I do as I am told, my back arching and my breasts thrust forward.

He takes the tub of ice cream and scoops out a ball, splitting it in two with his fingers he pushes it onto my breast and moulds it onto my skin. I immediately react to the cold, emitting a little scream and jolting with the shock then feel a warm sensation spread in my core 'Oh wow' I say and arch my back more as the ice cream starts to melt and drips crawl down my breasts. Becoming super sensitive, my nipples harden as Benedict ducts his head and starts to lick the trickles off. I feel hyper reactive to his caressing strokes as he attends to the most sensitive areas using the tensed tip of his tongue sweeping it round the underside of my breasts and the really soft skin under my arm. I moan, the feeling is both heavenly and torturous and he doesn't stop until it is all lapped off. Next he takes the melted chocolate and dips his finger in it 'Good still hot' he says licking it off 'just relax, the contrast of cold to hot will feel good, lie back a bit more.' I walk my hands further behind me and brace myself. The chocolate feels burning hot as he pastes it onto me. The warmth transmitting to my core and fire radiates lower inside me, moaning in pleasure, I can't believe it has this effect on me. Benedict takes two of the macaroons and presses in rings around my nipples causing a scratchy friction. I flinch a little at the coarseness. 'Stay still' he commands 'arch your back more and ride through the shock'. My body reacts to this breast torture, he maintains the momentum, increasing the pressure on my aureole with each circle. I thrust my breasts even further into his administrations, the feeling is painful but I want to test my threshold and keep pushing, the pain transmitting to searing heat within my core and my hips buck forward. He flicks my nipples with his fingertips then squeezes forcibly maintaining a tight hold. In his deep voice he orders 'come for me!' It tips me over the edge as I cry out, my body throbbing and I orgasm, light exploding inside me and radiating throughout my body.

'Oh, oh my god, how?' Gasping I throw my head back my insides pulsing, Benedict puts his finger onto my clit and presses side to side. More light shoots up my body and I ride a second wave of orgasm. 'Ahh that feels so amazing'.

As I come down from my high I look down the length of my body. My breasts are covered with sticky chocolate which has dribbled down my tummy and sides, Benedict, gazing reverently, still has his finger inside my panties and I feel so dirty.

'You - look – so - hot' he exclaims slowly.

I sit up, Benedict withdraws his finger and pulls it through his mouth 'hmmm this is my favourite desert' he says licking his lips provocatively.

His alluring chest is begging to be touched and my fingers twitch wanting to feel the firm muscle of his pecks covered with smooth hairless skin. I reach up and caress across his chest with one hand picking up a marshmallow with the other and dipping it into the chocolate I draw a heart shape on his torso. He watches my movements like a hawk, letting me have my fun as I lean forward and lick slowly around the chocolate outline. Then I lick across his pecks and circle each of his nipples with my tongue enjoying the sound as he groans in pleasure. I suck chocolate from the marshmallow and then pop it into my mouth chewing it while I put my hands behind his back and pull us closer together to give me better leverage, sucking hard and licking the rest of the chocolate off his chest, leaving red marks in my wake. I take in each nipple in turn and draw them into my mouth teasing the tip with my tongue and biting down lightly with my teeth.

'Jesus Christ' he says and more urgently commands 'Stand up I need more of you. Wrap your legs around me' and as he carries me to his bathroom I can feel his erection bobbing against my ass.

He sets me down next to his enormous shower, reaches in to turn on the water and removes his joggers, as he does so I step out of my shoes and panties. He pulls us both under the warm water, we kiss under the drencher head and let the water cascade around us. Stepping back for air Benedict squeezes some shower gel from the bottle, rubs it together in his hands and places them soapy onto my shoulders then starts to massage the lather in circles onto my skin. He works his way methodically down and around my breasts as I moan in bliss, it feels so wonderful, my body humming to the slow strength of his hands as they move and massage up and down my stomach and around my back getting lower with each movement until they brush down and around my pussy. My cunt reacts clenching wantonly, I start to feel the desire building in me again, marvelling that I could be turned on again so soon, wanting more, more than the last time. Benedict continues to rub the bubbles over the curve of my bottom and around the tops of my thighs, his fingers tantalizingly catching my folds each time they move around. He knows that he is taunting me as each sweep of his hand ends up pulling through between my legs adding the pressure of his fingers which only just touch inside my lips before moving away again. I want to grab his hands and hold them down there but he moves his massaging onwards and lower down each leg leaving me frustrated and needing more of the same contact.

Trying to bring his attention back to where it is needed most I blurt out 'I'm on the pill' somewhat desperately.

Benedict stills, stands back up and looks at me 'Are you saying what I think you are saying?' resting his hands on my shoulders.

'I am' I reply in my soapy state

He adds 'I had a routine medical two weeks ago and have the all clear, in fact I brought the confirmation letter back with me to show you, just in case this came up.'

Water continues to beat down between us as we hold our practical interlude.

'Thank you. I trust you. I was also tested and am clean, and as you know I haven't had the time to be with anyone else since' I somewhat tease, he raises an eyebrow which makes me giggle as I take a step towards him, back under the water and the bubbly suds wash away from me. 'I want more of you. I can't help myself, I need you. Is that so bad that I can't get enough?' I see his erection has reacted to my admission and is now full and straining.

'I have waited so long to hear that' he says 'come here.' Lifting me up my legs instinctively wrap around him, he slams his hand on a dial behind me and water shoots from jets in the wall of the shower. I am manoeuvred back and the surges pound into my shoulders and back.

He enters me, pushing his way in fully and starts to move gently inside. My body is bombarded with a myriad of sensations, the water jets assault my back, each time I am pushed up by the force of his hips one of the jets hits me on my anus and the feeling is surprising, it heightens the impact his thrusts are raiding on my insides, the blaze spreading in my core. My hands grasp around Benedict's shoulders, my fingers dig into the hard steel of his back and I can feel the ripple of his muscles as he moves in and out of me. The gorgeous sight of his tortured face concentrating on driving in and out, the drencher pouring down on his dark hair which slicks against his head and his blue eyes intense looking through me in between kisses, our tongues tasting and exploring.

'You are so fucking perfect' he says to me in rhythm to the movements he is controlling.

My head rolls back and I start to pant, crying out as I meet each one of his thrusts, still I need more and still he drives into me, my body taking every propulsion and encouraging further force and deeper penetration. I try to force his pace more urgently in the movement of my hips and the pressure of my hands on his shoulders but I am powerless against his might.

'Don't stop' I shout above the water 'I ..... want ....more'

He increases speed like a drum beating into me. It heightens the inferno of desire that is threatening to explode all-consuming inside me.

'Come with me' he demands and as he pushes so deep I feel like I will split in two, thud, thud, thud, fathomless inside me his body stiffens and my back arches as my orgasm soars through me and my world turns black, all I can feel is intense pleasure surging through me. For the first time I feel the full friction from his naked cock as it throbs and spasms and empties into me and he roars 'Fucking hell', my body pulses round him extorting every drop as his ejaculating goes on and on.

I am spent and as he lowers me to my feet, they give way and I nearly collapse on the shower floor. Benedict grabs me on my descent and stops me falling all the way down.

'Whoa there' he supports me out of the shower grabs an enormous towel and wraps it around me sitting me on the bath edge 'Are you ok?' He looks concerned into my eyes as he pulls on a chunky bath robe.

'I'm fine, sorry just had a moment, you must have taken it all out of me' I smile to ease his worry. Taking a deep breath, I know I'm ok, I stand up and into his inviting arms

'You're pretty amazing, you know that don't you?' he hugs me tight 'Don't ever leave me I don't think I could take it.'

My heart melts 'I could say the same.' He plants a tender kiss on my lips, grabs another robe for me to put on and pulls the cord firmly around my waist, like a parent would do to a child.

'Come on let me get you a drink' his arm is around me as he steers me to the sofa and sits me down. He turns round to find glasses 'Brandy?'

'Yes please that would be lovely' feeling cosseted I emit a little squeal of delight inside my head, my shoulders lift emulating a hug to myself. Sitting on his sofa wrapped up in his enormous cosy bathrobe I experience an overwhelming feeling of contentment that this gorgeous man wants to hang onto me.

CHAPTER 32

Benedict

Last night was pretty amazing and any little niggle of doubt I experienced over the last three weeks has been firmly erased. Not that I had any doubt that I adore Beatrice or that I want us to be together, it is more the fear of falling so quickly headlong into a relationship and putting my heart out there that I am risking the dread of being hurt again. Being together with her feels so natural, like cogs in the same clock, we tick along together in perfect compatibility and I feel sure this is the start of something special.

Whistling happily to myself I bound down the fire escape stairs, not wanting to wait for the lift, and stride to the coffee shop on the ground floor to grab pastries and cappuccinos for our breakfast. Then I run back up, two stairs at a time balancing the coffees in their holder in one hand and the bagged pastries in another, I have too much energy this morning and am excited to spend the day with Beatrice. Panting a little as I return back into my apartment I arrive just as Beatrice appears from the bedroom wrapped in one of my robes, her hair messy from sleep and her face not quite alert yet.

'I wondered where you'd gone' she said

I swoop over and give her a kiss on the lips. 'Morning my gorgeous did you sleep well?'

She looks at me, horror etched on her face 'Oh no!' she exclaims 'you taste freshly of toothpaste and I must have horrendous morning breath' she puts up a hand at me 'hold that moment – I must clean my teeth.' She turns back and dives into the bathroom.

Chuckling I turn to the kitchen island and lay out our breakfast, sitting myself at one of the barstools to wait for her to come back out sans morning breath. I enjoy a few sips of my coffee and grab my ipad to catch up on today's news.

A few minutes later she reappears looking a little fresher. 'Sorry about that, didn't want you recoiling in disgust at my lack of dental attention. Anyway' she joins me on the adjacent bar stool 'I slept really well thank you. Can't think why I was so tired.' She nudges me playfully then her attention is drawn to the pastries 'Oh my god is that a pecan maple croissant? It's my absolute favourite – can we share?'

'All yours' I push it towards her 'I wasn't sure what you would like so I bought one of everything.' Taking delight in being able to please her, I love the sight of her tucking into the pastry, the crumbs sticking to her lip and her cheeks full as she chews and coos about how delicious it is. I want to lick them off her but refrain from a repeat of last night, I don't want to smother her the minute she wakes up and she might like some personal space.

After breakfast, we hang out on the sofa, talking about our friends and sharing photos of our past lives from our phones, gradually learning more about each other. The morning passes quickly, I could happily spend all day like this but we need to meet up for lunch with Claud and Holly.

We decide to walk and enjoy the summer weather. It feels so natural holding hands with Beatrice, I keep looking at her as if I need to check she is really there and not part of a surreal dream. The warmth of the sun and the sight of her on my arm makes me insatiably happy and thankful to have her in my life. It surprises me when she pulls away and I'm hauled out of my joyful reverie, as we arrive at the restaurant. Then I remember we are keeping up the pretence that we are not fully an item, just yet. I know they all know there is something going on, but in the same way conversations with Claud have been more about his pains over Holly, I guess Beatrice hasn't had to the chance to be open with Holly either.

They are already at the restaurant when we arrive, sitting next to each other all dopey faced, looking into each other's eyes, focused only towards themselves and not seeing us until we are nearly upon them.

Holly shrieks when she sees us and leaps up, flinging her arms around her cousin and then hugging me like an old friend. Claud shakes my hand then kisses Beatrice on both cheeks more formally.

'It looks like you two have made up then?' I ask stating the obvious.

Holly gushes about their evening meal last night as we sit down, glossing over the fact that they had obviously spent the night together. Claud can't hide his just fucked grin, it is written all over his face, and he knows he can't conceal it from me. As I look at him with raised eyebrows, he ignores me and tries a diversion tactic 'I took the liberty of ordering you a beer'

Holly says 'And I thought you would be happy to share a bottle of white with me' oblivious of Claud's temporary discomfort, pouring some into Beatrice's glass before she has time to accept.

'Cheers' we all clink glasses and take a drink

'Here's to both our futures' says Claud raising his glass again making sure we are all looking at him. Then he clasps his hand over his mouth in mock concern looking to me as if to say *back at you Mountant.* 'Oh sorry are we still not admitting to that one yet?' and he looks tauntingly between Beatrice and I.

I look to Beatrice and teasingly put her on the spot asking her with an incredulous voice 'Oh something I don't know? Do you have feelings for me?'

Quick as a flash she replies smoothly 'of course, but only as a friend'

'Well then' I say 'Holly here and Ursula must have been very mistaken as I overheard them, as well as discussing my "Playboy" behaviour, swearing that you did have feelings for me!' We both look accusingly at Holly who smiles a little guiltily.

Beatrice pipes up 'Tell me then, do you have special feelings for me?'

'Good God no, well no more than friendly ones.'

'Hmmm' she says 'It seems Claud here and Pete must also be mistaken because I overheard them, while discussing my career obsession, proclaim you did.'

Claud also has the grace to smile sheepishly, shrug his shoulders and hold his hands out in defeat.

'That settles that then. They are mistaken and we are happy as friends.' I say

Claud speaks up 'Actually I have proof to the contrary' he pulls out his phone and wiggles it as if producing evidence. 'Sorry mate but I couldn't help it, you left an email open on your laptop and it caught my eye when I was walking past. I took a photo of it. It was addressed to Beatrice and looks like you were trying to get poetical.'

'Bugger you!' I say to him, mortified.

'But I never received it' Beatrice says questionably as if she might have missed something.

'That's because I didn't send it. I am rubbish with writing and I couldn't find the right words' I look to Claud imploring him not to show what I had written 'It was supposed to have been destroyed.' I put my head in my hands ashamed.

Beatrice laughing gently prises my hands away. 'It's ok. We can tell them.'

I look into my beautiful girl's eyes, which shine in happiness, confirming to me that there is no doubt she really means it and wants to share the news of our relationship with our friends. She gazes at me affectionately. I decide to show Claud and Holly in the best way I know how and plant a soft lingering kiss on Beatrice's lips. Holly squeals in delight.

Pulling apart and daftly grinning at each other Beatrice says 'I don't think there is any doubt now.'

EPILOGUE

Six Months Later
Beatrice

New Year's Eve

Messina Hall is lit up inside and out. A candlelit path guides the wedding guests as they make their way from the Chapel to the house, their flames dancing merrily inside their storm proof housings.

The bride and groom had gone on ahead to have the mandatory photos taken while their guests stayed seated and listened to an oboist perform a mesmerising version of 'Gabriel's Oboe' by Ennio Morricone.

Benedict, looking so handsome in his military dress uniform, is best man and had organised the ushers in strategic positions between the chapel and the house to make sure that all the guests make it safely inside withstanding the biting December chill.

As maid of honour, my duty has been trying to organise the three wayward bridesmaids, Holly's two god children and another cousin's daughter, all aged between 3 and 6. Despite their angelic appearance, looking totally adorable in their pretty cream dresses with ivy applique trim, they are devils inside and have little appreciation of the need to sit for endless photos. Armed with my remaining Haribo sweets, we only have a few pictures left to go before my bribery (and patience) runs out and the sugar kicks in. Then they can be handed gladly back to the responsibility of their parents and I will at last relax and enjoy the rest of the evening.

I am desperate to find Benedict and steal a few moments with him. We have been kept apart for the last 24 hours while he has been keeping the groom company (and goodness knows what else) staying at The White Hart in the village. They wanted to keep up the British tradition of the Bride and Groom not seeing each other the night before their wedding and today I have had to contend with viewing Benedict and his duties from afar.

Holly has dressed me in a very pretty empire line maid of honour dress. The bodice is made of cream lace over silk with a straight long chiffon skirt, it compliments my figure, skin tone and hair colour. I am happy not to be trussed up in something ghastly and she was sweet enough to include me in the decision making process knowing that I would have a strong opinion of what did and didn't suit me.

Photos done, I sneak away from the main throng of guests and grab a glass of champagne from a passing tray. My body senses a familiar presence behind me.

'You look sensationally beautiful tonight' I smile into my glass as I was about to take a sip and turn around. The sight of my gorgeous boyfriend still takes my breath away and I enjoy a panty dropping moment to gawk at him close up in his uniform, so sexy and all mine.

'Thank goodness it's you' I say 'I've missed you so much' we kiss and our lips linger close reluctant to pull away. Benedict raises one eye and seeing nobody in the periphery goes back for a longer smooch.

'How's everything going, Claud relaxed?' I ask once we tear ourselves apart

'Blissfully happy, on cloud nine, as you can imagine and today he loves us all, which is novel but a bit weird.'

I laugh 'are you ready for your speech?'

'Hmm don't remind me but as much as I'll ever be.'

'Ladies and Gentleman' Leo's voice blasts through the speakers 'if you would be so kind as to take your seats, dinner will be served shortly.'

'No rest for the wicked' Benedict moans 'I'll catch up with you on the table' he leans down for one more peck on the lips 'I love you' and he pinches my bottom playfully.

'Ow' I squeak 'go!' and I shoo him away unable to hide my grin 'I love you too' and he looks over his shoulder and winks at me as he is swallowed up by guests trying to find their seats.

Everyone makes it to their tables but remain standing, one of the ushers, delighted with his power wielding the microphone announces, 'Ladies and Gentleman please be upstanding for Captain and Mrs Claud Florence'

There is a round of cheers and claps as Holly and Claud, smiling joyfully, make their way around their guests to the 'Top Table'. Holly looks absolutely radiant, beautiful in her designer wedding dress I am so proud of her and bursting with happiness for them both.

Benedict and I, because of our respective roles, have been placed at opposite ends of the top table, having to endure further separation. Claud and Holly sit together in the middle along with Leo, Inno and Claud's parents. It is a narrow table but we are seated along one side so that we are able to face the guests and they us. We all enjoy a delicious 'wedding breakfast' then in turn Leo then Claud stand up to deliver their speeches. Benedict's speech by tradition is supposed to be the lighter hearted one with the opportunity to expose the groom's weaknesses and flaws in the most amusing but appropriate way. He does this with aplomb, totally at ease in the limelight, with a natural deliverance he has the guests laughing, groaning, clapping and hanging on his every word. Their rapturous applause at the end is egged on by the copious amount of champagne they have all consumed.

The cake cutting is followed by Claud and Holly's first dance and then the dancing continues until nearly midnight. Their plan being to 'go away' at the point the clock strikes to herald New Year; symbolic for their embarkation into married life.

Benedict had been busy decorating the 'going away' vehicle, an old military Landrover series 3, which he has covered in bunting and streamers and attached a 'just married' sign to the back. There are the traditional tin cans tied on long strings to the bumper which will rattle noisily behind as the vehicle moves off.

The newlyweds makes their way through the crowds who are clapping and cheering as fireworks explode in the sky. Just before she climbs into the vehicle Holly turns her back to everyone and launches her bouquet skyward over her head. She is not a very good thrower and me being closest to has no choice in catching the flowers before they land unclaimed and unlucky in a heap on the ground. I look back up in horror at the significance of my catching them, being the last person who would consider themselves in the running as next bride on the conveyor belt, but I have to steal myself and be a good sport hugging her and accepting the applause graciously, holding the flowers aloft and bowing to the guests.

The Landrover grinds and screeches as it is put into gear and Claud and Holly drive away to more cheering and well-wishing from the guests, then everyone slowly disperses.

A hand feels for mine as my fingers are laced with bigger strong ones. Benedict pulls me to him, my back against his chest and leaning towards my ear with an American accent quotes

'I really loved the skilful way you beat the other girls to the bride's bouquet' quoting a line from the Rocky Horror Show. I turn round and bat him with the flowers and he chuckles at me. He's holding two glasses of champagne in his other hand, giving one to me he says 'At last we can be alone, come with me, let's go for a walk.' It is freezing outside but still on a high from the wedding I don't feel the cold as I normally would.

'I am so happy for Claud and Holly, what a day.' I say as we wander around to the back of the house, he has his arm around my shoulders leading me in the direction of the maze. 'Where are we going?' I start to question his madness taking our walk outside. *Or is he wanting sex at our old spot in sub-zero temperatures?* As if reading my mind he takes his jacket off and puts it around my shoulders which I am grateful for.

'Don't worry I am not going to take your dress off out here.' He tries to reassure me leading me into the maze. It's a clear night and the nearly full moon shines brightly enough so we can see where we are going. We walk in companionable silence, I am at a loss as to Benedict's purpose, we take the familiar couple of turns until we find ourselves by the old stone bench.

I put down the bouquet of flowers and turning to Benedict I say light-heartedly with a little laugh 'At least not venturing in too far means we won't get lost in the middle of the night, between us we should be able to remember our way back out.'

I feel Benedict's mood shift, he appears suddenly serious in front of me, he chinks my glass 'Cheers' I say quizzically and take a sip. He is looking at me intently and for some reason my heart starts beating faster, aware something momentous is going on in his head. I have a moment of panic that he might being having second thoughts about us, then suddenly he drops down on one knee.

Looking back up at me he takes my free hand and says.
'Beatrice, I love you so much, you are my world. I knew you

were special the moment I first met you and I never want to be without you. Would you do me the honour of becoming my wife?'

THE END

BACK PAGE

Much Ado About Benedict

Beatrice, an up and coming corporate lawyer, is looking forward to a long weekend stay with her cousin Holly and her family, who are hosting a charity ball at their country house. Along with some extra house guests, officers from her uncle's regiment, she takes some much needed time away from her busy working life. On arrival she meets Benedict, a charismatic alpha army captain, but takes an immediate dislike to him realising he is the obnoxious man she had met the previous year. Inspired by Shakespeare's Much Ado About Nothing, Beatrice and Benedict's witty bantering is taken to a whole new level. Told through the eyes of the two protagonists, it loosely follows the play's twists and turns and explores their explosive sexual and romantic chemistry.

Printed in Great Britain
by Amazon